# OVERGROWN

# Overgrown

Luke Madden

*For the mystery*

# Part One

The Overgrowth job offered free travel and flexible hours. I didn't know much else about it. Overbrook got sleepier every year, and I thought if I didn't get out then I never would.

I saw Alex first. They wanted to watch an old sitcom, which I didn't like, but they quoted lines until they were gibberish and we were both laughing. We drank a pack of seltzers, then another, and I realized I couldn't drive home, or call a lift because my account had gotten banned.

They laid against my chest while I told them, facing the photo wall. That stillness always scared me.

"I get it."

"Yeah?"

"'Course."

I kissed their neck, hooked my arm further up their side. Slopes under my fingers, up, down, around. They held my hand to their mouth and kissed it. We came together, then slept.

Around 5 AM I sobered up, untangled myself.

"Think you'll ever leave?" I asked.

"Nope. My friends are here."

"Right." I wanted to steal a piece of the room. Commit something to memory so they'd feel I was there. "I'll miss you."

They nodded. "Good luck out there."

Overbrook rose through frost that morning. February had been cold, but the sun was out earlier every day. Shadows became sharp. I focused on the way: right, straight, right, left, left. Streetlights clicked off as I drove under. My foot lingered on the brake, crawling over intersections like a lame duck.

There wasn't much to pack. Renee had said to keep it as light as possible, repeated this in every interview. I assured her I'd limit it to the essentials, which fit into one suitcase. My backpack held creature comforts: speaker, hammock, eighth. Danny came by over two days to get the rest of my junk to a storage unit.

"You talk to Mom?"

"Of course," I said. "I think she thinks this is a fresh start."

"Is it?"

"Eh. Figured I'd see the country before I get too old."

"I hear that," said Danny. "Don't they have that rotovirus though?"

"You're thinking of something else."

"No, thought it was."

"Ok."

Danny and I didn't get together as much as we could have, which was why we stayed so close. When I got back we'd pick up the conversation from there.

Rotavirus would have been a blessing. We knew nothing about nothing out there. Walking in to tell farmers and rustics that their government would appreciate some insight. Allocate some funds, record some statements. The kind of thing that might take a week. But they insisted I clock all time to the 15th minute.

I subleased my apartment and booked my train ticket from Danny's couch. I didn't need to be in D.C. until March so spent the next five nights at dives adulthood had turned sacred.

Well Greased was our favorite because Kyle hooked us up. He started there the summer of his sophomore year in college — graduated summa cum laude in French, to his German mother's chagrin. Between tutoring and bartending he found the latter more agreeable and dropped any pretense that it was a side gig. The owner offered him a stake a few times, but he declined. Danny thought Kyle had plans for his own bar — this secret slacker just one idea away. I was grateful he didn't hold me in such high regard. It's hard to drink with someone of esteem. Every indignity they reveal is a slight against one's judgment. I preferred the Kyle that poured drinks, and Kyle seemed to as well.

I felt out of practice with his quirks, his slyness. He'd always had a thing for Alex, asked about them, and confirmed my departure date twice.

"You're so stone-faced these days," he said.

"Lot to think about," I said.

"Better here than here." He tapped the bar then his head.

"Yeah, yeah."

Nothing ran right there so Kyle was always holding together nozzles, stretching a foot to close a cabinet while reaching above like a starfish. It made me admire him in a way I didn't want to right then.

He fed me drinks. Told me about a buddy of his in Kansas, homesteading. She figured it was better than corporate life, that the food grew itself by now, and it did. The real trick was the forest — it sprouted when she first got there, a couple elms way out by the pond. Few months later they took the pond. After that they blocked the road, trunks cracked right through the asphalt so she had to weave through fields to leave. They

4

hadn't reached her home yet but during the day she looked out to that black forest floor and saw it shift and swallow.

"Bullshit," I said.

"Yeah, just wanna keep you here." He laughed.

Mornings were gray at Danny's. The linen curtains above the couch had faded from a pastel yellow, shading the white walls as the sun rose. One foot hung off the side with the other propped on the armrest. Those last nights kept me numb.

I showered and left $50 with my key on the coffee table. The door shut and instilled a panic I'd never gotten used to. All bags on one side of the door, the only way through to slingshot to some other place. The flight was exhilarating, but I had no clue where I might land.

The National Overgrowth Environmental Response (NOER) office in D.C. was stacks of white papers and black binders over five perimeter desks shared by an intern, a slight man with chewed cuticles, and a woman in earth tones. Humidity baked the papers until the smell was sopping, like books left out in the rain. Howard shook my hand and apologized — the building manager refused to turn off the heat until April. In the back was a massive whiteboard with little red notes over a calendar. They weren't usually this unorganized, he explained. Each day corresponded to an Atomic Habit that would make them a well-oiled machine. I expressed appreciation for his vision.

"That's why we liked your interview. You see what we're trying to do here."

"Of course, thank you for the opportunity."

"All these claims? They're just words right now. We need real accounts from one of our own. Do you remember the COVID pandemic?"

"Sure, mostly watched YouTube with my brother. We were pretty young."

"Ah, well back then the government released a ridiculous amount of funds to anyone that could sign their name. But when the dust settled people like me and Renee were finding where it actually went. We won't make the same mistake twice. Most of these problems can be fixed with some minor adjustments anyway. Yes, the whole thing's a mess, but I believe we can be smart about cleaning it up."

The intern set me up with a work OnBoard to complete tax forms before signing it over. They explained all the recording I'd need to do before any funds were sent. "'Unnoticeable or unreasonable management' is the rule," they said. "Otherwise Howard might bounce it back and I have to ask you to go back out there."

"Sure, I get it. Have you ever gone on the road?" They chuckled off-beat and glanced over my head.

"Maybe one day! I think it'd be really cool to see it you know? But not now."

"Right, right."

A quick tap on the door brought us around. Someone was poking in, gave a nod to Renee then called out to Howard. "What's the status on reimbursement?"

"You're covered, don't worry," said Howard. "Let's take this opportunity to introduce you two. River, this is Orion — your senior on the trip."

They stepped in and were taller than I'd guessed, limbs disproportionate with their torso and neck. We shook hands. They smiled tightly before crossing their arms.

Howard said Orion and I would be the eyes and ears of the office, while they were the internal organs, beating away to keep things moving — our office just another organ in the body of government. When we kept the arteries clear, it could run. He went over the reporting process once more and then wished us luck.

Orion walked on while I grabbed my bags. After loading my backpack, Orion stepped out of the driver's seat and tossed me the keys. "You'll drive the first few hours," they said. "I didn't get a lot of sleep." The SUV smelled of cedarwood and sweat, with cracked leather seats. An old hybrid without self-drive. Orion had a bucket hat over their eyes by the time I started the car. Our first stop was Wynne, Arkansas, a million miles out in the jungle.

We would blow in for a few weeks, teach them a thing or two, move on. A little routine. But I couldn't imagine living there. Even before Overgrowth. The solitude was what got to me. In towns of five or three thousand, everything and everyone became a known quantity. Why stay?

Howard had said Orion would fill me in on resident procedure. Their legs were up on the dashboard. I thought better than to say anything. The road flattened out and narrowed to two lanes leaving D.C.

We curved around bare mountains to head southwest through the valley, keeping the Appalachians on our right. Semis grazed in a line under cotton balls of grey. The tree line flew in brown blurs between rolling hills, the car just a white noise machine. I imagined driving over every green knoll, gaining enough speed to launch us over the range, then winding through switchbacks to Morgantown: a mythical land where they used furniture for firewood and went blind from drink. The sun sunk below the visor, so I reached over to the glove box.

"Hey! What're you doing?"

"Do you have any sunglasses?" I asked.

"No. They're in my bag."

"Ok. Can you drive for a bit?"

"How 'bout we find somewhere to sleep."

"Sure."

There weren't any deadlines on claims. Whatever we didn't finish would roll over into next year. No pressure to work longer than eight hours, which included a one-hour lunch.

"This is my car, you know," said Orion.

"Right, I know."

"Ok, so don't go through stuff before I've shown you."

"Got it. Sorry about that," I said.

"It's fine, no big deal."

Hill Rise Inn faced I-81, with rooms looking out to a sliver of mountains. The attendant preferred cash. Orion asked me to take care of it while they got their bags. I stuffed the receipt in my backpack for whenever I learned expensing. Rooms 6 and 7 tucked into the top corner, opposite of where we parked. They wished me goodnight at 7 PM.

The matted, dark green carpet reminded me of the ones in elementary schools, the kind that soaked up sweat. The sheets were worn but fresh and matched the curtains. A farmer overlooking a winter night hung above the TV. I dropped my suitcase onto the luggage rack. It groaned then collapsed in two snaps, shooting wood across the room, splinters nailing me in the ankle. I cursed and fell to the ground. The pain died faster than the noise, but I massaged it all the same. Orion crossed my window without glancing in. All the pieces were in the corner when they crossed again, then once more with their bags, to the other side of the lot, to another room. I chuckled, then found my speaker. People are people.

On top of the sheets, feet to the farmer, I reviewed the day. The way over, what I said, how I said it. *Stonefaced.* The album looped. I got up and shook from side to side, bent down to touch my toes, left to right, right to left. Chest to the sky. Did little kicks to loose the gunk I was making. From the windowsill, there were more than mountains. Blinking red dots framed the range, with yellow spots clumped around their base. I cracked the window and asked for a cosmic album. Smoked what I had. Over the plain, out to the range, my mind soared, with the crown of my head cutting the air, slipping it off my fingertips. Suspended at a good altitude, I flipped back, watching the sky rotate through its celestial sphere. A couple shouted in Room 5 and I checked the time — 8:58 PM. The door slammed open then shut, then open then shut, and the fight continued in the courtyard. A biting crescendo with no rests. My ankle pulsed and I fell to earth, pushed to move. Stepped out.

Through the underpass, a deluge of bright red and yellow signs shone. But I was drawn to the wooden one with green lettering — Millhouse Roadside. A plastic menu with maroon stitching contained the totality of the human experience: ten entrees. I ordered a double when the reality of the day came into focus. The desolation of the road stretched before me. I ordered a round for the pair at the bar.

~

10

My ankle came back first, a collapsing pain. Room 6 was underwater, deep below the waves, and I was on the seabed. The nightstand floated around. I closed my eyes and when I reopened them some of the water had drained. The current was strong and knocked me down before I could fully rise. The bags were packed, apart from the speaker. Taste of decay in my mouth.

I had an hour before we were back on the road so dug out my bath bag and got to work. Pieces of the night clarified what the job was — an exercise in freedom. In thirty minutes, I had the key in an envelope and slipped it into the return slot. Orion waited on the edge of the hood with their knees up, eyeing the highway. They nodded at my approach and stepped up to the driver's seat. We were on the road forty-five minutes from when I had surfaced.

"I'm sorry I was an ass yesterday," they said.

"You're alright."

"Thanks. Just been a shitty week."

"I get it, no worries."

They grew up in Kentucky, near Lexington. Their backyard was a thicket that they, their brother, and sister, made a kingdom. When they got TV, it became a stage. High school was rough. A scholarship got them out to South Carolina, where they met Jordan: a nature freak that convinced them to work summers at the Salmon-Challis National Forest in Idaho. Working the park wasn't as romantic as Orion pictured, but it

11

got them outside and paid enough. When Jordan proposed, it felt right, and they moved over to Richmond. Orion had been substitute teaching when a parks buddy told them about this job three years ago, and they had worked it ever since, taking the winters off for Florida. Jordan lived in Richmond while they were away, pouring cement with their team until it got too cold.

Their left knee leaned against the window while they slouched back, cruise control at 60mph. Towns got sparser and denser, concentrating whole communities into a few blocks. In between, wheat fields pushed against the March chill, fragile wisps that begged to be put out of their misery but would instead grow and grow and grow to be strong, then cut down. The clear sky was stifling, more than any overcast.

Orion pointed at cows and claimed them as theirs. They said all mine were dead after passing a cemetery. I tried to play but they said horses didn't count for anything, only cows. Their jeans were a decade out of style, straight cut and boxy. Music was all over the place. They didn't reference celebrities or cultural phenomena except the pandemic, and even then only grunted about it being rough. Older than me, definitely. Somewhere between 30 and 50, placid.

We wound up the mountains then down, and up, and so on. Orion checked their OnBoard while driving down, the sticky quarters, nickels, and dimes of the cupholder clinking fast. They glanced when I grabbed the bar above me. *You too?*

They cut someone off outside Virginia.

"Fucker," they said.

"What'd they do?"

"They were taking forever. I just gave them a gift."

"Oh yea?"

"Yeah. There can't be any more good in the world than evil. So getting cut off by me is better than whatever else might've come their way."

"Huh."

"And now they're due for some goodwill, to keep it even."

It was the kind of logic I heard in bars. In these ways I think Orion entertained themself, because the rest of our drives they spent running their fingers over the door rest. People reacted, insisted on answers Orion was ready to provide, so we didn't talk much.

Towns crowded in the basin of the valley where we stopped. We got two rooms at the western cusp. Orion was on a different floor. It took a couple pickups before one of them would sell me weed. Always cheaper than dispensaries. The bag had a cartoon fish smoking a joint on the front, with "OVERGROOOWN" across the top. Leaves burst out the sides of the paper while they used both hands to keep it all in. It tasted sweet and left a tang in my mouth. The surrounding area had big houses running up slight slopes onto big lawns with lights that were always on. It reminded me of Philadelphia, and I went to bed with the TV on.

I drove us back up then down the mountains until we flattened out in Tennessee. Orion slept. The roads were empty. For a few hours I counted mile markers, then Beyond the Borders. When that got old, I filled in the plains with calamities. The sky was open and could accommodate any meteor or nuke or flood. Didn't trouble myself with "what next." A car passed and transformed, stretching into a ship that took off into the sky. During the COVID pandemic, Mom drove us around with the radio off. Danny and I rattled the cage for a while before softening on the view. She'd tell us she knew a secret path to the country, always one turn away from the wilds, and I'd said there was no such thing, that people had gone to the Pacific Ocean and there was nothing out there we hadn't seen except space. Wilds we knew were hedged plots out West, ever-shrinking. There was uninhabited space for crops and fields, but our world was known, even more so from our tablets; yet never without worlds to discover as we delved into virtual sandboxes. Worlds vacant of humanity, borrowing only the necessities — caricatures to create improved worlds. But a dissonance remained, the limits. On the road that would fade as the mind wandered, but it was like painting with one's palm. So the imagination sandwiched itself between the two, comatose.

Dreams could bridge the two but were unreliable, and I hadn't dreamt for a long time. I wondered if Orion dreamt. Not sure how they could with the torn leather pushing needles into our backs, boiled by midday sun. Their back curled toward the window, right leg to chest to rest their head. An impulse to jerk the steering wheel or make a grab at the glovebox ran through, something to disturb them.

The sun was setting just outside Knoxville when Orion told me to pull over. The 14-room shack had movies on Thursday nights, which I attended after downing a couple shooters I had picked up from the charge station a few hours back. It was an old superhero movie, and I laughed harder than I needed to, which made the couple and family there laugh. The couple was on a road trip through Appalachia and the family had been evicted one town over. I offered the dad a couple shooters and he accepted, so I didn't pity them. When they left, I chatted with the couple a while longer before one of them got a text and said they needed to go. I felt nosy that night and watched them slip into Orion's room.

They were behind the wheel the next morning. We stopped in Nashville for cowboy hats and whiskey. They had played "Tennessee Whiskey" a couple times before I suggested the detour. My hat was tall and tawny while Orion's was snakeskin with rivets running through the sides.

"So, you don't know what we're doing?"

"No!"

They laughed more than I had seen them smile. The hat slipped off their head until the attached string caught around their neck.

"What did Howard tell you?" they asked.

"That we're interviewing claims and sending videos of the ones we think are legit."

"Guess that's close." Orion ordered another round on my tab. "'Assisting as necessary.' Should've been in the job application."

I nodded.

"Well, that's 90% of the job. The other 9% is driving. If you're lucky, you'll run into some real damage you can get money for. Plants don't care. Might hate the moss in the bathroom, but it doesn't obscure any windows, obstruct the room's use, or pose any health hazard, so no dice. A backyard forest's the beauty of rural living."

"So what's 'assisting as necessary?'"

"PR." They took their shot, so I took mine.

"As in?"

"Weedkiller, sheers, boiling water."

"Doesn't it just grow back?"

"Yup."

"Fuck."

"Let it rot."

16

Orion didn't think anything was impossible. In fact, everything we imagined was more possible than what we couldn't, but because we'd imagined it meant it wouldn't come to pass. Their whole life nothing had turned out how they thought, for better or worse. The more Orion tried to predict, the further it slipped, so it seemed better to leave things. Nothing was more destructive than hope — it shot through every happy ending.

Outside of Nashville were two strips of road through nothing. We hit Memphis in the afternoon then passed over the Mississippi into Arkansas. Tankers crowded the western bank like siege weapons. I'd seen videos of the burn teams but never gave much thought to their supply. Their midnight suits with the angular, white trimmed sleeves were a fashion staple, imposing and clean.

The fields past the bridge were charred. Tufts of green broke up the black mounds, signaling an imminent burn. Soot settled on the car before Orion washed it away. Smelled like a bonfire. Heat with no source. Remnants choking the air. In West Memphis, the thickets started, then grew to forests, with weepy branches that threatened either shoulder. A topiary tractor upturned in the ditch. The creep enveloped houses, factories, roads; the exception being those that stayed. Shadows watching behind curtains of vines enveloping their porch. Their daily life burning, and cutting, and stomping, to keep a living room. Treading that path. I wanted to know their sense of place.

Furthest I'd ever lived was a summer in Key West, bartending and sleeping with six others. Danny had a friend that hooked me up. The tips were shit and the sand never left my suitcase. The crew was good; one of them had a bong we hit before every shift, another did gymnastics. She opened to cute tourists by faceplanting, giving us a chance to introduce ourselves, *where're you from? how long you here? oh we're just down the road.* The next summer they all wanted a bigger house. Two of them would bring partners. We'd lost steam over the winter and one of them dropped early for an internship. I did clerical work for a lawyer that summer and got out at 3 PM every day.

Ahead, a wall of brown trees broke up the fields. The road cleared a cavity in the ribcage, tunneling along. We hugged the median around corners, hoping no one shot out the opposite way. The light was fading, and I squirmed in my seat, unsure if I wanted to get out or keep driving. We came to a one-light intersection. Lawns overtaken by shrubs and ferns framed either side and ran borderless until the next street. Orion turned off to the outskirts of town, to a one-story strip with 6 rooms: Wynne Nights.

A woman in floral print stepped out when we pulled in. Orion threw it into Park and screamed. They ran up and hung their arms around her, squealing. The woman laughed and shook or nodded her head to every question.

"You must be River." Her hand was wrinkled and firm.

"Yep. Nice to meet you."

"You too — I'm Marijean. Let's get your bags."

My room had a loveseat perpendicular to the bed, facing the kitchenette, with a coffee table between. On the far end, below a wide window, was a dresser adorned with bobbles: a steam train, a red plastic lizard, a vase, and the figure of a woman carved into stone. In the center was another vase filled with orange, yellow, and purple wildflowers that reached eye level. The curtains were heavy and brown, crimped to either side. I dropped my bags onto the loveseat and went to sleep.

We had to see the mayor, let them know we were there and going around. Susan Withers' office was early century modern, clashing minimalist whites with wood-framed photos of horses and Native tchotchkes.

"Orion. What a surprise."

"Did you get my message?"

"Yes, we just expected you later."

"Ah, well, guess we made good time, huh?" Orion bumped my elbow.

"Yeah," I said. "Didn't stop till we saw trees shooting through windows." Susan chuckled.

"Oh yes, they grow tough here in Wynne. But folks seem

to be managing alright on their own."

"Of course," said Orion. "Which is why we're excited to give them the resources they need."

"Well, that's the federal government for you: always ready to pitch in for the cleanup." I forced a laugh.

Orion dropped me off at the first claim, downtown. There weren't any rental cars available, so we split claims between Wynne city and Wynne County. I had been through the training sim a few times on the road and thought I had a handle on deflection. But the PR part stumped me. Orion only had one battery powered hedge trimmer, told me I'd need to find a tool for myself and expense it. So I stood straight and flexed my hands.

Linda Howard answered the door after the third knock, incredulous. She brought me to her living room, covered in a layer of fine grass and weeds.

"How often do you go in here?" I asked.

"Every day. It's the living room."

"Right." I picked up a vine silhouette of a chair. There were holes down to carpet where the feet were. "Was it always like this?"

"Alright, you should go."

"What? No, I know it wasn't like this before Overgrowth but if—"

"But yeah, I was outta town for a couple months, so

yeah, it grew into the least used space. I get it. You'll take some photos, and I won't get shit, right?"

"I don't know, you—"

"So you think I can get some money. Or someone will actually deal with it."

"I mean I can help—"

"Yeah get outta here."

Those were the claims I came to value. Contempt for someone like me but not me. No harm done. The subsequent homes hadn't submitted claims before, so I dumped boiling water onto the vines and grass and shrubs, and they thanked me on the way out, asking once more when funds might be distributed. I reminded them the office needed to verify, and they remembered, but if I knew when that might be it would be helpful, and I didn't, and they thanked me again. Every claim was in a "low occupancy space," so nothing was coming.

I stomped my way to the door of what I decided was the last claim of the day. The photos were of a basement bathroom, where moss crowded the wall opposite the window — everything but the mirror would be covered. Plants left mirrors to preserve incoming light. Lloyd Dower wouldn't see a cent. A kid answered.

"Hey, is this Lloyd Dower's place?"

"Yes."

"Great, can you get him?"

"No." They pushed the door in a bit. "He's taking a nap."

"Ok. Can you tell him that a NOER rep came by?"

"Yes. Thank you." They shut the door.

I waded back to the street, then walked to the intersection cornered by ditches. The main road was east, but I couldn't remember which way that was, so I started straight. Flat homes sheltered under a procession of trees, blocking landmarks. A few cars passed and asked what I was doing so I told them who I was. Two of them asked if I'd check out their place and I said we would if we had their file. One of them insisted I go see it then, so I told them I was late to meet Orion. I knew I was going the wrong direction but figured wherever I ended up was as good a pickup spot as any. On foot Overgrowth seemed more manageable; instead of reigned into one lane, worried branches might break through and shred glass down my face, the weeds parted at my presence and leaves guided the way. I found a restaurant and messaged Orion.

> *@ wests bbq. pkup?*
>
> *fnd ride? bsy*
>
> *ltr?*
>
> *ok*

The red and white checkered paper in the baskets had a reassuring crinkle. I talked to the owner of West's over brisket. Any Wynne restaurant without a liquor license went bankrupt post Overgrowth. Bars felt better to eat in anyways. He took a liking to me and pulled a higher shelf whiskey for the second round.

Orion had finished early, and Marijean made them dinner — roasted salmon with green beans. Marijean offered leftovers but I was full.

"How was the first day?" asked Marijean.

"Lot of 'piss off,'" I said. She laughed.

"Yeah, that's Wynne. Won't have much patience for BS."

"Thought this was the 'City with a Smile,'" I said.

"Doesn't apply to bureaucrats, honey."

"Didn't think of myself as one, but I gu—"

"Oh Marijean, did I tell you about Lou's new dog?" said Orion.

"No! Where did he find it?" asked Marijean.

They had moved onto Lou's new shed when I slipped out. My things were in my bags still, and I wanted to take them out even less. I drifted around the room, brushing my fingers on furniture and paint bubbles. Closer inspection revealed it was still a motel room, despite the homey touches. A Grizzlies fan recommended a spot earlier that day, which I considered as I slid down the wall left of the window. But it was probably a sports bar. The thought of my OnBoard coming to life when I crossed the threshold rooted me to the floor. The screams to buy beers and wings and tokens. Must have been twenty minutes or so before a knock at the door. It was Orion with a box.

"Hey, Marijean insists you to take leftovers." They handed me the container.

"Oh, that's sweet. Tell her I said thanks," I said. Orion looked past me, into my room.

"We're staying here, you know," said Orion.

"I know."

"So you can unpack."

"Right."

They shook their head slightly and looked up. "You need a ride into town tomorrow?" they asked. It had to be an hour walking along the highway.

"Yeah, if you could."

"Sure. Be ready at 7."

"No problem."

We usually left around 7:45, but I was always ready at 7.

Northwest of downtown was a shop filled with plants. Vines interlaced each shelf and grew bushier toward the top where sunlight hit best through unadorned, wall-high windows. It was further than Central Market but less crowded, and the shopkeeper didn't mind if I read the magazines for a bit. The glossy pages were tactile and generalized compared to the ads I usually got, and there was a reassurance in choosing to consume them.

"Where do you get these?" I asked one day.

"They're easier than you think," said the shopkeeper. "Cost next to nothing to make these days. Practically give them to me. Maybe $10 for the whole rack." I whistled, he nodded.

His name was Yates and owned the shop since he was twenty-six, being forty-one now. His buddy was supposed to go in with him until his sister got into trouble in Salt Lake City and he had to move out there. Yates scrounged together some loans and opened Town General a few years later than he'd have liked. He said this and most things in a conspiratorial tone, through the brush of fiddly figs, with little nods that I found myself mirroring while paging through *Glamor*. I knocked the stand down one day and Yates kicked me out and said I could come back tomorrow. "I can't be pleasant today," he said.

No other store had plants. If there were plants, it was those that had slinked through the door or burst in corners like mold. A charge station clerk swore by water and bleach, and she sprayed the entire store every couple hours. *Good excuse to move around.*

Wynne was a hollow of a place, surrounded in branches and shadowed light. It was chilly, but the ground knew heat, stored it in the knolls that ran from the Mississippi. Mom used to say knolls were giants' graves. But mountains weren't graves, mountains were churches. So when we drove out to them in the summer Danny and I would kneel and "pray" which cracked her up. They must have drunk from the Mississippi, floated out and away to the Gulf when they heard us coming. All rivers were giant highways because they all led to the ocean. Yates and his buddies used to float down a while, with these little koozies around their beer cans with their own floaties, so they'd slide them to one another like skipping stones. That was before they all left, before Overgrowth. They had teased him for being Mr. Business Man but didn't anymore. I heard them chat sometimes in Town General and was glad to hear how he lit up. Wynne moved slow. The giants must have felt Overgrowth coming centuries before us, took their time burying their dead and vacating. I slept better in Wynne than anywhere.

The cool weather made for nice walking in between the chopping and boiling and sweating of claims. So flat out there, cloudy days swelled into mountains, silver-blue and rich. I stepped into a ditch concealed by the brush and imagined the town was deserted, left to watch the clouds and be consumed. Time to burn. Before bugs really woke up and a breeze still bit.

Orion was better about picking me up after the first day and even bought me dinner a few times. Only a few of their claims had been closed. The car reeked of cigarettes, so maybe they just drove around, smoking. Marijean hosted more dinners and I think had chided Orion for not inviting me because they made a point of reminding me the morning of and while picking me up. Guests at the motel were infrequent, and almost always someone from town in a situation, so Orion and I talked even less in the parking lot. We understood a need for solitude.

If I saw anyone I had "helped" at West's, I left for the night. The first time I stayed Lyle Waters bought me drinks, pitching a riverboat business, a lucrative affair I could help him break into. I'd just need to call in some government favors.

One Saturday, I ripped up prairie grass behind the motel, then laid down on my stomach, resting my head on my hands. The bit I'd ripped was like hair, tangled and soft. It lay perpendicular to how the rest curled in the wind, milky roots frayed. I spent an hour like that, eyes on the clock. The sun made it above the tree line and warmed my back. I scooted a bit to the left so the patch could get some. A couple frogs croaked back and forth in their hideaways; insects buzzed louder out there in that watershed. By the third hour, the new blades were as tall as my ring finger.

My OnBoard pinged. Again, and again. Images and media and messages. All pleading I check out their claim next. Yates. I'd given him my address the other day and he must have spread it around. I took it off and laid back.

When I woke up it was getting dark and I couldn't find

the patch I had ripped. I smelled chicken and remembered Marijean had promised a whole bird that morning.

Orion was waiting on the couch when I came in fingering a tall, round chess piece. I made a show of taking a big sniff, laughed. They didn't react, kept feeling the piece. "I hate eating," Orion said. "It's constant and a pain. I hate sleeping, water, trimming my nails. I just want to live, but everything gets in the way. You know they say Satan was attractive; he loved the flesh. I didn't get that until I grew up, couldn't understand why it was bad to love the body, to love beautiful people. It's a prison. We're supposed to be more, above all this shit."

By the third week, Yates invited me fishing. I asked him what the buckets behind the counter were for and he unveiled the tub of *wrigglers*. After feigning too much interest, I was on the hook for 4 am the next morning.

Orion squinted when I told them, but I couldn't tell if it was their usual squint until they mentioned it to Marijean.

"Oh, well you have fun now, stay safe," said Marijean.

"What?" I said.

"What?"

"Is he a psycho or something? I didn't have an excuse."

"No, no, nothing like that. Yates is a good man," said Marijean. "Just off."

"Doesn't seem like it."

28

"People talk, you know."

"Not really."

I'd tried inebriating myself after failing to fall asleep early, and I must have passed out at some point, but it didn't feel like it, as when I woke up it was still dark outside and the lamps were on. A couple birds twittered back and forth in the black. No dreams. Yates was arriving soon, so I got out of my clothes from the day before and into some long sleeves and jeans. Yates recommended extra layers against the sun and mosquitoes, so I added another shirt and already felt stuffy in the cold room. Too early for music or media so I sat in silence and let it stretch. Mom had Aunt Heather take Danny and me a couple times in the Delaware River, on the Jersey side where they didn't check for licenses. I took to it well. The current pulled my line out further than I could cast. Perched on a rock, motionless until the first jerk, then yanking up, snapping the line. Aunt Heather retied it every time, even when I did it on purpose to see if she would do it for the umpteenth time.

Headlights passed over the curtains and I felt a sudden panic. Worse than a psycho, Yates could be a nuisance, one I was locked in with for at least six hours. As my only friend in town, it'd be a hard loss. Turning off the lamp came to me a second too late.

Yates was still behind the wheel, media off. The road was dim and dimmer with his headlights. Back through the winding

29

wood, where branches apparated then cut across the windshield, we turned off to a single lane. He picked up speed.

"This bit makes me nervous," he said.

"Why?"

He shrugged. "Seems too solemn. Like you're not supposed to see the end."

Yates took up the oars to the rowboat as the mist formed. He put his back into each swing, scrapping us across the water. Another dinghy set off across the lake silent and glassy in the dark.

We shared our first fishing trips. I told him about Jersey, and he told me about Missouri. Every summer his dad took him to the Boston Mountains in the Ozarks. They considered themselves mountain folk in spirit and birthright. He knew the Boston Mountains weren't the tallest or longest in the country but knew they were the most beautiful, as no other used water like they did. West Virginians and Coloradans had told him as much. But one girl or another he ended up in Wynne. He figured people in Wynne never forgot the Missouri of him. *Plains folks.* But they were kind, even when they found you strange. At least that's how they treated Gary, the last weirdo he'd known in Wynne. Gary wasn't around anymore, except in the ways that mattered.

Yates then retaught me to bait a hook. Our journey had been choppy, made worse by my hangover, made worse by lack of sleep. But sitting in the middle of the lake the sun was only beginning to rise so the bugs slept, humidity a spirit. It smelled filthy and alive. I wondered if Yates had ever been irresponsible.

My line plucked the water to a ripple, ringing out. For so long I worried Yates might say something, but we sat. The mist curled off the surface, up to brush my face, cool and wet.

I threw up over the edge of the boat while Yates laughed. The sun had turned everything nauseating and bright, emphasizing the bob on our wooden island, and the thought got into my head so there was no way I wouldn't. The boat tilted with me and I considered jumping into the murk inches from my face. On the drive back I kept the bucket hat he lent me low over my face while he reenacted the scene with increasing color. We went to Town General for some *hair of the dog that bit you*, which I refused, but Yates insisted was a post-fishing tradition. I wandered among the foliage while Yates sat on the counter. Thumbing through issues of *Vogue*, sipping on our beers. A painted "Gone Fishing" sign in the window. I followed a spider plant's tendrils around the grains. Each strand spawned a mini version of itself, cascading in clumps over rice onto the floor where the ends were trampled and wilted. I tucked them under the aisle with my foot where they would get less sunlight but avoid a boot. I found the original near the endcap further from the door, guarding the spatulas. The deep green of the center

31

evoked a wilder, ancient time.

"How long have you had this one?" I asked.

"Hm?" Yates finished his beer and walked over. "Oh, haha, her. Wily little thing when I got her. Must be 6 years now." His voice was far away, serene. I pointed to a rubber plant growing through the magazine rack, and Yates sauntered over, pinched the tips of the burgundy leaves. We went like that for another six-pack. Gary had given him three of them.

"Yates, who's Gary?" We'd broken into a pack of ice cream sandwiches and sat on the floor by the freezers.

"Oh. An old friend," said Yates. "He's not around anymore, except in the ways that matter."

"Right, you said that."

"Ah."

"Is he alive?"

"No."

"I'm sorry."

"It happens."

Gary was born in Wynne, though no one could recall him as a child. Perpetually fifty. Yates met him at a fundraiser for the middle school, after a tornado destroyed the gym. Gary examined each raffle item before writing his bid. Several times he picked up and shook pieces before Reba Waters shooed him away. Yates and Gary were the only two there without kids. Yates admitted he was trying to drum up business; Gary had only come to win raffle items.

That's when he started patronizing Town General. Yates needed business, so he made him feel at home. After his first visit, Gary walked directly to each item he needed. When he asked about magazines, Yates got a rack. That kept him around a bit longer, sometimes even picking up mints or a chocolate bar. Yates was proud when he asked for bait and could reach around for the bucket. That's how they got to talking. Gary mocked Yates' gear and setup. He'd said he must enjoy the peace of fishing because that's all he would get on the lake. Yates called him a low life with nothing better to do. Next time Gary went in he had a plant. *You need to differentiate your store.* Yates had a few he kept behind the counter, so Gary set the giant fern next to the door, beside the baking sheets, which he told Yates to move because people thought about baking when they were buying flour, not when they were leaving.

Befriending Gary cemented Yates' status as a weirdo. Alone in the store, Gary revealed a sharper tongue than he let on, eviscerating former schoolmates and cousins. Despite it, he was fond of the town and never wanted to leave.

"What's funny is they think this some special place," he had said. "Like there's something in the water or bluffs. Never know the place is dull as dirt. Never realize that it's them. It'll die with them too. Then it'll be some new place." Yates didn't consider much of what Gary said except that it buzzed around

33

in his head. Once Gary predicted the end of the world, down to the date and minute, and Yates couldn't remember when but thought it right.

Gary came in with a bag of dirt the day he told Yates he was dying. He asked him to use that bag as it had a good mix of nitrates that would bolster the philodendron's growth, his body he intended as fertilizer. Yates cursed him and told him to leave, which Gary did. The next day he asked the same.

"I hate how that fucker talked," said Yates, against the fridge. "Like he knew the whole goddamned story."

So when Gary did die, Yates did as he instructed and buried his remains in a long terracotta, the same that rested above the cheese section of Town General. The philodendron wrapped around the store three times.

"I know it's nuts," said Yates. He was drunk. "He was dead, I could've not. But he never asked a thing of me. That was it. Fuck. Maybe we'll go under."

I found a small clearing off the road and felt the warmth, a gentle crawl. The grass brushed my knees, which I coaxed into a mat, down among the threads, weaving green. Felt myself a giant watching forest tops in the breeze.

The weight of my arms became apparent, so they drooped to the side, then my perched knee, the clenched hips; a fallen sigh. Here, maybe here.

Awoken by the chill, staring up at the head of my silhouette. I stepped out carefully to preserve the shivering outline of my shape.

I ran into Susan Withers a few times at West's BBQ. She always had a salad, and once invited me over to chat. Progress was good, or as good as it could be, Marijean treated us well, no, I wasn't sure when we'd be finished.

"How are you and Orion?" she asked.

"Good. We have dinner, split the car on weekends."

"They get into town much?"

"Maybe on the weekend."

"Sure." She grinned. "So, what do you make of them?"

"They're nice. A little reserved. Comes with the job I suppose."

"Huh. Always thought of them as quite outgoing."

"You think."

"Oh I know."

"Well, sure," I said. Susan laughed and poked at her salad, shook her head.

"You're no fun," she said. "Anyone tell you that?"

"Nope."

"Maybe after a few drinks... Oh don't look like that. I was your age. I get it. Just stay out of trouble."

"So what's your beef with Orion?"

"It's a small town — people's business is their business. I don't ask, just observe. And I've observed some disturbance when they come around. That's all."

"Sure."

"God you need a drink."

"Right."

Marijean gave me the gist. Last year, Orion had an affair with Susan's sister, Claire. Susan wouldn't have cared one way or another if not for Rachel, Claire's daughter. Orion and Claire spent weeks holed up in the motel, sometimes leaving in the dead of night for God knows where. Orion didn't say a word about it to Marijean — stopped talking to her all together. Because Orion was going to stay suspended there a while. Because Wynne knew whose care was whose in that lot, and Marijean would've had to ask about Wilson in all this.

Wilson was an all right guy — got with Claire after she dropped out of school and moved home. He was sweet to her, and she always liked the strong ones.

Toward the end, Claire brought Rachel around, introduced her to Orion, and they hit it off pretty well. Claire got it into her head that this could be their loophole, that Wilson could be open to some arrangement, like they could all come together through her poor daughter. Then Orion left, and the two fought all over town.

All Horowitzes were back under one roof, but Rachel

36

was seventeen so wouldn't be for long. She was quick and had the sense to apply out of state. Claire and Wilson were rarely seen out together, but both cars were in the driveway every night.

I pulled their file and sure enough it had been marked that year. Orion assigned it to me. The Horowitz residence was just outside town. Orion took the day off when I requested the car to go out there and asked I drive them into Memphis. I watched the burn team on the way back, striding through smoke in their insulated suits. Grouped together in their deep blue they looked like a bug zapper lasering the field.

Rachel answered the door and called for her dad. Wilson was about my height with massive forearms that held both sides of the door. I blurred through my spiel. He grunted in amusement and turned inside, went through a glass door across from the living room. I followed to the backyard where he stood by a shrub. I poked around when he didn't explain and found the cellar door. Moss covered the steps down into a bog basement. A frog leaped through the opening into the water, unseen. It climbed out onto the broken stairwell across from the cellar opening, above the algae and lily pads.

"Have at it," said Wilson.

Yates whistled when I told him what the rain boots were for. He threw in his old fly-fishing overalls.

I yanked while a bucket of roots floated alongside. The fibers slapped my forearm, slipping water in under the glove. It ran clean the way mud does, the smell of which drove me mad. Spores leaped out of lily pads along the turquoise walls, veins pulsing around the shimmering pool. The frogs were friends in that they climbed onto the driftwood near me, placid. If I reached out they dove, barely a ripple.

Rachel came down the second day. Spring break moved plain those days. She sat on the cellar steps while I grabbed weeds, asking me questions about the East Coast. Schools in the east were better and farther, but Arkansas was cheaper. The Horowitzes had visited Chicago years ago and Rachel took to the edges and concrete, places built by and for us. Cities were a numbers game — the more numbers the more people. Pulsing clumps where no one knew you.

She pointed to where the water came in. Behind the broken stairs, an armoire covered a hole. Wilson made it three years back looking for a pipe. Nobody knew where the water came from, chalking it up to an unending well. Anytime they pumped it out the basement refilled to the same level.

"Have they told you about us?" asked Rachel.

"No," I said. "But I know."

"It's a real fucking mess."

"I know."

"What do you think?" she asked. I stayed bent over the bucket, nodding to a song in my head.

"I think you shouldn't think about it too much," I said.

She laughed sharply. "Oh wow, thanks." Then she left.

Orion's "Completed" photo from last year looked like a flooded basement but with fewer frogs. I had a quarter done after two days.

A red slit ran a few inches down the inside corner of my right wrist, raw. It ached to the touch, deeper than skin, the crust of a scab failing to knit itself. I noticed it after fishing with Yates. Could've been from leaning over the side of the boat, all that wood. Or maybe a hook skimmed along the surface. But it wasn't closing up, and I'd seen infected — this wasn't. Red, red, no movement, no blood. The ache. When I did dream, white tendrils pushed through and linked around the base of my thumb. They stretched with my arm, latticed the palm to brush the tips. I'd wake up before they got much further.

Marijean made pasta with zucchini and lemon. She had me chop tomatoes then lay them out on a baking sheet for salting. My technique was awful, wasting time. She bent my fingers to a claw, which she said I would get used to.

We were the only residents that week and spread out around the kitchen, taking up space in the adjoining lobby. Marijean stayed in a lot of hostels way back when and wanted something similar in Wynne, though calling it one would never fly.

She moved into Wynne Nights a few years into running it. Felt like she was taking care of her home and guests so that every bit of good living was good business. Didn't make getting by any easier, but the two were no longer at odds.

Bonfires still happened but weren't the communal space they had been. Most of Rachel's friends moved at the start of Overgrowth, *Memphis refugees*. Now the fires were her and the other five high schoolers grabbing whatever wasn't nailed down, feeding it higher and higher so they were sunburned and drunk by midnight. She only really got along with two of them, but the worst had moved out.

School had a couple in-person classes, like gym. Otherwise she went over to her friend's or her friend went over to Rachel's and they sat in bed, running lectures. More of a nuisance than anything — designated time to sit and daydream. Though she wanted to get her grades up that semester and next so she had an excuse to daydream in another state. Schools loved Overgrown kids, plenty of scholarships.

Mornings into town got brighter, with a sweet scent that made coffee offensive. A bloom came on that filled the emptier parts of Wynne. We passed one of my makeshift trails and for whatever reason I pointed it out to Orion.

"Do you walk the same path every time?" asked Orion.

"Not always. Often," I said.

"Sounds boring."

"Nah." I wanted to describe it, that when I knew it was when it got interesting. There was always some new branch in the way or bird calling out. Or it was a slow week and not much had grown but the season had progressed. All these tiny buds a little further along than the day before, obscuring more moonlight, more sunlight. The best was a couple days after a storm, when everything was knocked around and surged. Or nothing except such and such truck was on the street instead of the driveway and the lights were on inside and silhouettes were moving around and the place felt more real and unreal — so simple it seemed staged. But none of it would make sense to Orion, nobody, because it was what wasn't there, what suddenly was, what had changed, because you had to keep both spaces in mind at once and the only way to do that was to have moved through it. So they'd need to walk with me to get it and I realized it didn't really matter if they got it, they'd get it some other way.

I went into the store and Yates looked out of sorts, reserved, like I wasn't there. The refrigerators hummed and hummed while I thumbed through Farmer Weekly. A co-op in Albuquerque had raised funds for a new harvester through sim tours of the fields. Yates was gone when I looked up. A mom came in with her two kids, so I got behind the counter and greeted them.

The girl hid behind ferns and jumped out at her mom and little brother when they got to the end of each aisle. "Jesus Christ! Mary Louise Sullivan so help me I will leave you here!" She ran, squealing, tipsy through the next aisle.

The mom finished with her daughter's forearm in one hand, two steaks, asparagus, and small potatoes in the other. The register had a pin so we waited a moment, two, before she took it on an IOU. She marched the squirming girl out, forgetting the little boy rubbing a leaf between his thumb and forefinger. When the door shut he looked at it, then me, confused. I waved, he waved. Then he toddled forward with the leaf and was out to his mom. Town General was quiet, and I leaned on the counter with Farmer Weekly, imagining days slipping by like that — a store clerk, a zany boss. I had been more the bussing, coffee-making type, but figured there were transferrable skills. Maybe I had some franchise ambitions too, a media campaign about the resilience of small businesses in Overgrowth. The hour stretched, then the shadows. A beat tapped with my fingers, over, over, over. I stepped out and was sad to feel a chill. The warmth had passed. I poked a root system by the door with my toe and thought I saw where it led: a bur oak, alone on the plain six miles west, breathing further and further.

Yates came back after another hour and thanked me for watching the store. He realized he hadn't fed his cats that morning and knew if he didn't do it then he'd forget the next morning then the next and they'd starve. I asked for media of them so he projected them around the store. One of them was chunky and laid on her side the whole time while her brother flicked a toy around her oblong body before it hit her eye and she screeched at him and chased him through the aisles.

"She acts so cranky, but when Bubba got sick she'd poke him to play and cheer him up," said Yates.

"Bet they really love you." He chuckled.

"Oh, maybe. I love them though."

I realized I had worked on my day off.

"How do you get a job like this?" asked Rachel.

"Be good with people."

"You know any architects?"

"No."

"I think I could do that. There're too many ugly buildings."

"Takes a lot of math."

"How do you know?"

"Just what I've heard."

A door slammed and Rachel straightened. Wilson called for her. She met him in the backyard, and they started arguing. She was supposed to charge the truck; he shouldn't make her charge it when he drove it most. My bucket stayed full a while, and a while longer, and I figured the best approach was direct. I waded my bucket over to the concrete steps then grabbed the cellar door handle with both hands, peeking. Rachel was in his face about leaving the truck running. I stepped out with half the door, but they didn't flinch, so went back for the bucket. It was heavy and I worried about my back. I felt the sun on my neck, heard a CRIICK, BOOM, then more shouting while the whole place went tipsy black, a breath smacking all over. The weeds pulled down, filled my nose with pond water. Light showed through the murk, but I was moving further from it to the hole under the armoire. Someone caught and dragged me up. They were shouting at me and I wanted to shout back because I didn't want to be there anyways.

"Fuck this," I said.

"Headdress plinko log mousse," said Rachel.

"Agh."

Rachel snapped in front of my face a couple times, so I slapped her hand. The water had gotten over Yates' overalls and soaked me; I tried to get up. They dunked me until I flailed. I vomited upon resurfacing. They screamed at each other again.


Orion arrived at the hospital an hour after the first stabilizer, all slams and stone.

"Are you ok?" they asked.

"Yes," I said. "Wilson and Rachel were great."

44

"Where is he?"

"I don't know."

"Did he do this?"

"No." I overheard Rachel explain to the doctor how they were arguing, how he cursed me for leaving the door open. She did a great impression of her dad, whistling the "w"s and chewing the "sh"s. Orion studied me then left. They veered to the visitor area, and I followed.

"No!" I heard Wilson.

"Oh yea!" Orion covered the ground between them in two strides. They jutted their chin and finger up at him. "You have any fucking clue what you're doing over there? No, seriously I— hey!" Wilson grabbed his coat and made for the door. Staff circled Orion but didn't pursue them outside.

"Hey!" yelled Orion. They kicked a rock his way. It skipped across the lot in three bursts.

"You're fucking nuts," said Wilson.

"Oh fuck off."

"Orion," I said. "He didn't do anything."

"Stay out of this," they said. "What Willy? Wanna take it out on some kid? Big tough man yea?"

He slammed his car door then made a big arc around us before cruising away. I was tired and sat in a visitor's chair next to Rachel.

"You need a ride?" asked Orion.

45

"No, Mom will get me," said Rachel. They nodded and glanced away.

The claim was rescinded the next day.

The days got longer and smelled of grass. After three days of stabilizers, I was cleared to work on claims. I'd forgotten to ask about the cut on my wrist that still burned. Howard made a joke about suing before reminding me about the waiver form. I'd visited every claim but needed to check each untreated one once more before closing out. There was a ranch being dragged into a pond, a barn hidden in a young forest, a McMansion beset by deer. These were the fringes of Wynne, haunting sights to waste a day walking. Lloyd Dower was the only one in town. The grass grew higher and thicker since my last visit, obscuring everything below the gutter. I caught my breath on the stoop, noticed the bursting "Dower" mailbox. Mail people are nobler than me. I waited a while before knocking a third time.

"What?"

I jumped up and away from the ghost voice. A kid pressed their face to the screen of the bay window. I collected myself from the ground.

"Is Lloyd Dower home?" I asked.

"No," they said. Half their face was blurred by the mesh, the smell potent. A sense I was seeing something I shouldn't.

"What's your name?" I asked. They stepped back and

shut the window. "Hey! I'm just following up on a claim."

They opened the window. "The fascist regime has no authority to subsidize their mismanagement through stooges!"

"Ok. But you can get money," I said. "You guys have been living here, right?"

"Yes!"

"Then you can get money. Your Dad just has to show me around."

"I can do that."

I shook my head. "Needs to be someone who's 18."

"I'm 18."

"No." We watched each other.

"I'm coming back tomorrow, around 6," I said. "Will he be around?"

"Can you come Sunday?" It was Tuesday.

"Sure."

They shut the window, their OnBoard light disappearing. I sat on the stoop for a minute before they yelled at me through the closed window.

Marijean knew of Lloyd Dower. The mom died a few years after Grayson was born. Lloyd worked tech from wherever he was, usually Memphis. He enrolled Grayson in a remote program when they were old enough, when kids still ran across the yards. He believed Overgrowth was a federal tactic to seize the remaining private farmland from rural Americans.

"Wouldn't be surprised," said Orion.

"You think?" I asked.

"Ha! Yeah, and Howard is heading up control implants." They took a bite of their mashed potatoes. "Just saying: the government finds their opportunity."

"Not sure he wanted a kid," said Marijean.

"Right," said Orion. "But he has one. And they're clearly neglected. River, Renee can get you in touch with child services."

"Orion."

"What?"

"River — don't make a mess of it."

"He doesn't even want them!"

"Until you give him a reason to fight."

"God, Marijean, no." Orion sat back from their plate. "Grayson's terrified in there, fed and clothed by Drops, and you want to turn a blind eye." Marijean's face tightened.

"I *want* Grayson to live their best life. Now whether that's with their dad or not isn't for me to decide."

"Which is why we call in a professional."

"Professionals like you all?"

"Like someone that knows kids."

"If you could, would you give out more money than you do, River?"

"Yeah," I said.

"Right," said Marijean. "And I'd hope you wouldn't send

48

this plague upon us to get a little more land. But hey, who's to say."

"This is nowhere near the same thing," said Orion.

"Yeah, 'cause we have no idea how it'll go," said Marijean. Orion stood. "I run a motel for Christ's sake! Kids can scream and claw so bad you think they're possessed. They get in that car and you think they'll shatter the glass with how they throw themselves against it."

"It's ripping off a bandage," said Orion, quietly.

Marijean shook her head, looking far away, straight back. "People know Lloyd. They know he has a kid. River stumbled on the worst-kept secret in Wynne, and all you want is to force some other bureaucrat's hand so you can ride out feeling good about yourself. Do whatever the hell you want, I can't stop you. Just remember you don't live here." Orion gripped the back of their chair, staring down the gravy boat. Marijean got up to clear dinner. When she came back for the second load Orion was gone.

On Sunday, I found a path to the Dower house. It wound from the road to the front door in an arc, trampled. Lloyd was clean-cut and long. I showed him the image of the reported area and he laughed. "Buddy, look around," he said. "It's brought its bags and set up shop." Thickets blocked the front two rooms, maybe family and dining, with books, albums, porcelain, and monitors stacked on the long table. A small path snaked to a back room that glowed blue under the door, two more curling to the bathroom and kitchen. Another went to Lloyd's room, trampled. I imagined Grayson, smaller than they were, brushing past the branches as they grew higher and higher and bloomed and brought bugs. I started in the basement with the moss.

The bathroom was spongy underfoot and cool. No sign anything was below the swampy surface. Yates had dug up an old tool belt which he charged me exorbitantly for, as I had asked, and we sent the bill to D.C. The paint scrapper was great for an initial pass, finished with weedkiller or boiling water; an awning of green coming toward me, crumbling, revealing soft tile.

"How long will this take?" Lloyd asked.

"You have somewhere to be?"

"Don't we always."

"Never seen it this bad. Could take a while."

"Sure." He sighed. "Listen, if I give you access, can you get it done without me here?"

"It's real bad. Whole place is overrun," I said. "How'd it get so much of the house?"

"Oh you know, boiling frogs and all," he said. "Can you do it without me?"

"Of course. Might get done faster though if you point it all out to me."

"Yeah, but I've got plans, bud. You're clearly great at your job, so I'll just stay out of your way."

I knew he just wanted out, but the compliment still lifted. I wondered how many had the same apprehension relieved. Persuasion that made you feel more capable than you were.

"You know, you can get a lot of money I bet," I said. "They might even buy the house outright." His eyebrows popped.

"Oh yeah?" Both feet in the door.

"Yeah. You been using all these spaces?"

"What's that got to do with it?"

"Overgrowth only occupies unused space." I quoted the manual. "If a room or place is abandoned, it is ineligible for reimbursement."

"Figures," he said. "I've gotta be everywhere at once or Uncle Sam thinks it's his. No, I don't use the downstairs basement regularly."

"What about upstairs?"

"Well Grayson is always messing around up there."

"What about you?"

"I'm in and out."

"As in?"

He opened his mouth then paused, cocked his head. "I work in Memphis." He laid each word carefully.

"But your room and the front rooms. It grows fast, but

if you're in there at least once a week they usually won't bother you."

"What are you getting at?"

I furrowed my brow, looked confused. "I just need to make sure they've been in use for when I write the report. Have you been using those rooms at least once a week?"

He looked around, bobbling his head. "You know, there might have been some weeks in there I couldn't make it back, you know how it is."

"Ah."

"But my kid's around."

"Ah. Well they don't count, being a minor."

"Right, right," he said. He spoke slower to figure out where he was going. "See, their mom died a while back, and money's always pretty tight. You close with your folks?"

"Yeah."

"They both around?"

"Dad isn't. Passed a while back."

"So you know," he caught. "You've got to be independent. You've got to be more than a minor sometimes."

"Sure."

"And it's not like how we grew up, you know." He shook his head. "Their whole world's online: school, friends— hell, church! I know parents whose kids don't leave their room all day, and they're happy as can be. Just expect us to slide a meal under the door. Don't even think where it comes from, or who's paying for the roof over their head."

"Right."

"It's selfish. Like we're supposed to be at their beck and call, but only when they want something. Rest of the time we're supposed to shut up, 'cause god forbid we contradict them. Kids have all these protections, but think the government cares when an adult shoots up in a ditch? It's heartless."

The moss breathed in our silence, bloating.

"I could've lied," he said. "Could've said I've been here the whole time."

"Would Grayson?"

He threw his hand up and walked out, reared back. "Y'all are more deranged than I thought if you're going around having kids call the shots. You know they have a distorted sense of things. They didn't grow up like we did." And the rest he seemed to say to himself because he was swearing and pointing around the basement while I stood still there. I started going with the scraper again and forgot about him like he forgot about me. Until a long silence and I turned around and he was staring at me.

"Oh, get the hell out."

I wondered what I would be like with a kid. I sighed.

The claim was rescinded.

I started to rethink intelligence because I was sitting out

watching the figs grow and when I stood in their way they angled around me as best they could, which I chalked up to evolution at first but realized there wasn't much of a difference between what we did and what they did. We only put a name to it, and if we thought about it too long we chose what was bad for us, stayed in the shadow. They ran wild and only chose their best outcome, so maybe they were smarter than us.

My favorite sim as a kid had you befriend a beast — horrible with its slack jaw, dissonant wheezing as it pulsed on three spindles. If you didn't read it right it surged to your head, cracked in three snaps. The sunken red slits darted too fast; the careful steps had no rhythm.

When I figured it out I was enslaved, unable to stop our dance, everything a reinterpretation of this shared breath. I could master it when I chose, but this required constant posturing, exhausting and addictive. It bled into my dreams and conversation.

We closed the last claim on April 26th. I drove around and tried to recall a house I had really helped. Yates smirked when I told him this. *Nothing to help.* He hoped for a buyout but figured us being there meant it wasn't coming. So in some way he never wanted to see me again, and we laughed. He gave me a small pesto jar filled with dirt and a cutting.

The smell of my room had mixed with my things and

reminded me of the beach, of Mom. I ran my fingers along the walls to internalize the paint bubbles. Packed in ten minutes.

Marijean made us a lemon loaf, drizzled with icing, baked through with the divine and poppy seeds.

We meant to leave at noon, but I was kicking rocks at sunset. Orion came out and wouldn't look at Marijean but hugged her, thanking her for everything.

The light dropped when we broke into the bluffs, toward Memphis. Yates had meant to take me out there, said there were ancient trees as wide as school buses were long, growing into their own forests.

Memphis glowed ahead and made me feel like a castaway, oblivious to what I had considered basic. Orion watched the road. We had to put some miles behind us.

A creek in Overbrook dried up when I was ten, which I didn't get — water went on and on, part of a cycle. I called Danny a liar, said he must have blocked it further up, so I followed the muddy trail all day until it got dark and figured it was safer to find the source than turn back. I learned it never got dark-dark, that things were only gone when I closed my eyes, that even without a moon some glow gave colorless shape. Then it was all the same: the trash bags, dead birds, branches, and traffic cones which tripped me up under bridges, along the banks. I walked and clung to roots, toward the source. Sloping up to a lake I didn't recognize a trickle ran down the rocks and died before it had a chance to flow. I got out of the creek to see where the block was but couldn't find it. Twenty feet of dry grass separated the lake from the creek. I crept back in, near the trickle, and bashed a rock around the source to loosen it up. This only slowed it, and I panicked, having sealed it up permanently and ended the cycle, then dug with my fingers to free it until the tips bit in the wet cold but found nothing so I sat and cried because why was I out there.

"They were separated when I got there," said Orion.

"What?" We were switching places in Missouri, after coffee, and they said this as we passed each other.

"Claire and Wilson," they said, shutting the passenger door. "I know you know about us."

"It's not my business."

"Yeah. But Wilson's a prick, and I'm sorry you had to deal with him."

"He was alright."

"He's a prick."

"Alright."

They sighed. "You don't know what he'd say to Claire. It's why they separated. Everyone seems to forget that though. Like I split them up."

The road was packed with semis and pickups. Orion said it would be bad for a while, getting around St. Louis. My right hand on the wheel, noticed the raw red slit, switched to the left. On either side fields ran wild in the spring rain.

Orion met Claire at a rugby game. Orion wanted something to do between claims, Claire coached. They got dinner after Orion's third game, on the pretense of giving Claire tips for a game they didn't even know the rules for. *Natural athleticism, baby.* They got around to her separation from Wilson, sleeping on her sister Susan's couch. He was good to Rachel. Sex was good too. But his face set and he changed the subject whenever she talked about history or music. She talked fondly, loudly of college and regretted dropping out. Later he'd find laundry lying around or a dish in the sink and lose it. Orion recited poems in bed, tugging Claire's hair on lines they liked.

They were at West's BBQ together, at Claire's insistence. Wilson approached the two and asked Claire to step outside. When Orion rose he asked they stay put.

"The nerve of that fucking guy," said Orion. So they were yelling in the bar, then yelling in the lot, then Wilson smashed Orion's windshield.

"I egged him on, for sure." They chuckled. "Next day Susan had the sheriff take him in for a bit."

I glanced over, raised an eyebrow.

"Oh, Susan would sooner have me pick daises in a lightning storm than be in Wynne. But she fucking hates Wilson."

Susan thought nobody was good enough for Claire. But Orion was temporary. Orion and Claire had time in the motel. They cooked and let weeds block out the windows. Then Claire turned despondent thinking of Rachel. "She should've just packed a bag and left. Settle in somewhere else, then get Rachel there and through school and she's home free." Whether it was time or a kid, Claire and Wilson got back together before Orion left.

"'Oh, you don't understand, he's just protective of us.' Christ! 'He acts out because he's afraid to lose me.' Fuck me. The grip that man has on her, it's disgusting." They shook it off. "So, now you know."

A semi's billboard on our left blinked ice caps then deserts in rapid succession to advertise a cooler. I waited until it was far ahead, then a little longer.

"Did you see her?" I asked.

"Yeah. They still fight."

# Part Two

We were on the road up to Iowa when I had my first series of dreams in months. I hadn't picked up weed since Virginia and was tired after a day of driving. I brought a wooden chair out to a ditch and angled it up at the sky. Marijean came over to get me to help slaughter a goat. She insisted she needed it for the music and I was selfish for not helping. The chair dipped forward, and I was drowning in the lake before Yates pulled me up. Claire was in the boat with him, and I got the impression I was intruding, so I jumped back in.

There was another dream I couldn't recall, one that woke me up in a cold sweat. It was still dark, but I could hear birds. I found a pack of cigarettes in my bag and smoked three, curled up against the headrest. When the light came in I remembered

Yates' gift and felt guilty, like I would choke the cutting. A friend once swore by bong water for their plants. I took the fourth and fifth outside.

Orion came out of their room across the parking lot while I watched the sunrise. They tilted their head and gave a small wave before jogging in the other direction. We were somewhere north of St. Louis, following the Mississippi from a distance. I thought of Alex — when I left their place for the last time. We weren't in touch, and starting things up felt pointless. I finished the pack and crawled back to my room, under the covers, under the pillow.

The last dream was a memory of Alex and I's trip to the beach in Jersey, but it was Orion. They said I ask too many questions and should leave it alone. I asked what to leave alone but they just repeated themselves again and again until they were screaming and screaming to get up, what the fuck was I doing, we had to go, hello?! and I hit the ground hard and slammed my shoulder against the door before opening it.

"Woah, are you good?" they asked.

"Yeah, yeah, what's wrong?"

They searched my face. "It's 9:23. Are you ready?"

"Shit. Give me two minutes."

"Sure." They hung their mouth and looked off.

"Thanks."

I swung the door and ran to the bathroom first. Whipped

my dirty clothes into a pile then my bag. Had to have been under a minute, but Orion was waiting behind the wheel.

The left side of the passenger seat had a bad piece of cracked leather, so it was best to cross my legs or angle against the window. But I could only hold the pose for so long before needing to shift, bearing the scrape to loosen my right side.

"Some advice," they said. "Don't let them see all of you."

"What?" I said. They sighed when they thought I should know something.

"Show up when you say you're going to show up, stay in shape, ask questions, and people won't look further."

"Oh."

"Yeah, 'oh.'"

"I'm sorry I was late."

"Yeah, yeah."

Clouded sky stretched. It layered, darker in the distance, with holes that shot out slanted, golden beams.

"I was sober," I said. "This morning."

"Okay."

Up a hill we saw the Mississippi, sleazy in the gloom. Green enveloped a bridge so the forest reached across the strait, connecting Missouri and Illinois with a webbed umbilical cord.

"What were you doing?" said Orion. "This morning."

"Had a smoke," I said. "Couldn't sleep." We dipped

below the tree line and lost sight of Her. "You run every morning?"

They nodded. "River, they're looking for something. Any excuse to discount you. Because however bad they are, you have to be worse. So do it all: the things they want to do *and* try to do. Do it better than them. Then they can't touch you. So yeah, I run."

The Spencer mayor had an impersonal touch I found comforting. We had a house stocked with pots and pans and pale red flowers in the corners. Orion offered the master bedroom. The bedframe was mahogany, and wilted vines climbed each post to drape overhead. The blinds were drawn and taped. Orion gave me a lamp, but I refused to live like that. Sunlight warmed the worn wood floor. I placed Yates' cutting in the windowsill. He said it would be a while before it needed to be repotted as they got along growing from the nodes of the last piece, which I found charming. The double window faced the front yard, sloping down to the street. At the end was a ditch, full of topiary shaped by the wind. To the left an elm stretched in the breeze, leaves twittered. I imagined calling to someone on the lawn. *I'll be right down!* Motels had made me nostalgic for childhood.

There was a solar-powered weedwhacker in the garage that I tied a string around and hung out my window to charge so it wouldn't get eaten in the grass.

I walked toward the center of town. Unlike Wynne there were sidewalks, and the roads were coated with layers of asphalt that shined in the coming heat. Trees were spaced uniformly in the neighborhood, once trimmed in the same fashion, now haunted by unique spirits, scraping the sky. Though the tallest couldn't put a dent in the great void above. It wheeled overhead, a bright blue dome. Between identical roofs the horizon flew. I felt I'd walk off the edge soon. It had rained on the way in, and I flicked leaves while passing under, took a whiff of the wet, green mush.

At night, I walked. Coverage was spotty and the thought of going from work to a sim was miserable anyways. So I walked one path until it looped into another, until it brought me to a bar. I stopped in for a drink or two then hit the trail. If the sky was clear I'd take a joint to a field and lie back. A couple times I saw a shooting star. The first week was always the most frightening, until the desolation was comforting. I could breathe knowing I was surrounded by empty homes, hidden among the thickets. The mosquitoes were bad but I pretended not to care until I didn't and they were only a reminder that I had a body.

"Really, I might keep them if the coloring weren't so garish," said Denise Perkins. Her posies decorated the east wall in shades of lilac and tangerine.

"Makes sense."

"That's the bend in the Earth I suppose."

"Right."

The flowers hung loosely off the vinyl, twisted into some sturdier vines so the vase petals could reach higher, bloom. I stomped a small space out of the shrubs to get at the wall. I grabbed handfuls and ripped down curtains.

"Oh, if I'd known they were that weak I may have just done that myself, haha!"

"Happy to help," I said.

"Now it may not have gone that easy if I had. You know how it is."

"Sure."

"Bend in the Earth, you know."

"Not exactly."

"The curve of the Earth?" She raised an eyebrow. "Yeah, shows what they teach these days." Denise sighed and leaned against the corner gutter. "It's what made this whole Overgrowth. You think the Earth's some perfect sphere?"

"Probably not."

"Right. It caves in a bit like a crater at every spot this has happened. Means we're more connected to the Earth too. So weird things happen. Why you think they call it 'bent out of shape?'"

"Figured it was when something is supposed to be some

other shape."

"Right, but where do you think they got that from?" She gestured around her yard.

I nodded then pointed inside. She followed me in, detailing why the Overgrowth cover story existed. The tap was slow and there wasn't a cover for the pot. She mentioned the weather rays that I must have heard of and worked the same circle when I said I hadn't. I lapped boiling water onto the side of the house while she got around to the lizards.

"Now I'm not saying I believe any of this, but it does seem awfully convenient, you know?"

"Uh huh." I yelped when a splash came near my face.

I yanked the shriveled roots and dug out some bushes that she thought got into her foundation. I took videos for the team and got my things.

"The other one's still out back, I think," said Denise. I drew my lips back. Orion had never joined me on a job.

In the backyard they sat in a lawn chair, dictating to their OnBoard. They were squat, with real glasses. I waved my hand in front of them, and they jumped. I spread my hands out.

"Hey! Sorry," I said. "Did Howard send you?"

"No." They sized me up. "Who?"

"I'm part of the National Overgrowth Environmental Response team."

"Oh," they laughed. Sat back in the steel chair. "You a

flat earther too?"

"Ha! No."

"Then why're you letting her say all that nonsense."

"Because I'd be the idiot to fight her on it." Their laugh was quick and biting.

"Not much of a teacher, huh," they said.

I shrugged. "Maybe if I was ever going to see her again." I thought about it. "Maybe not."

Sci followed me to job sites. At Denise Perkins' they asked for my list of claims, figuring they would yield more dynamic samples. I refused, maintaining confidentiality, so they drove around looking for my rental truck every morning then asked the homeowner if they could assist me. They were a second-year grad student at the University of Illinois Urbana-Champaign, getting their masters in natural resources and environmental sciences with a focus on soil. Overgrowth was a mixed bag: in Missouri it was in the water, in Nebraska the pollen. But Sci believed it started in the ground and based their thesis on it.

"Because we're at a bend in the Earth, yeah," I said.

"Nuh-uh, no spreading misinformation. We ag scientists put in too much work for that."

"You're an ag scientist?"

"In the research sense, yes."

"Sheesh." I pulled crabgrass from cedar cabinets. "Imagine you have a worse rap than us."

"Why? We just investigate possibilities."

"Yeah, but don't people blame you all for this?"

"I wouldn't."

"Because you're an ag scientist."

"Because I understand science."

"As in?" The grass had woven a dead bedding of itself, under which the wood cracked.

"It's a series of choices, discoveries, that helped us feed the world and gave us leisure. It's centuries of work by people who knew they'd never see the literal fruits of their labors."

"And now we have this."

"Sure, but people talk like it's a conspiracy. Or a greedy corp fucking things up. They can't accept that they asked for this. And now we're trying to fix it."

"Y'all have no clue."

"We never do. Science is about finding the pattern, not knowing it. 'Cause once you know it, means there's a million more you don't know."

They had their legs crossed in a wooden chair with a rounded back, next to the bucket I dropped grass into, so I went between kneeling before them and the cabinets.

"We just force things to interact sooner than they would have," said Sci.

"Assuming they would have interacted at all."

"Well why wouldn't they?" They were getting excited.

"Because we're pushing things together. OnBoards wouldn't have just materialized."

"But assuming we're not gods that's still a natural interaction. Nothing you see, touch, or taste is *un*natural. That word's meant to distinguish what we can pick up in the woods and what we pick up in the woods then combine with something from the lake. We're just as much a part of nature as anything else, so anything we do *is* natural."

"Seems a little simplistic."

"It should be."

They spent hours scrolling their OnBoard in silence, then would whip around the room yanking weeds and humming. Familiar in a way I had forgotten.

Orion was on the plush green couch when I came home. They ran their OnBoard and chatted softly, involved in a sim. I tried not to look, for fear of them moving to their room. The chatter kept things warm. I heated the last of Marijean's meals — salmon with kale — and split it onto two plates, setting Orion's on the coffee table on my way upstairs. They nodded then did a double take, asked me to talk.

"So how have things been going?"

"Good," I said. "About the same as Wynne. Bit more

passive aggressive."

"Good, good." They closed the sim and set their OnBoard on the coffee table, then broke up the salmon with their fork. I kept my plate on the tips of my fingers.

"How about you?"

They nodded with their chewing. "Good, all good. I had this guy try to get me to call Howard today so I called an old buddy and we gave him the runaround."

"Oh yeah?"

"Yeah," they laughed. "Told him we'd start pulling bank statements, IRS, the works. He shut up fast."

"Can we do that?"

"No way. He was a prick though," they said. "Your food's going to get cold."

I took a few bites and sat back.

Orion once got stuck in the middle of a plain. Their SUV hadn't been acting right for a while and gave up for the night. The stars stretched in a smoky wisp. The cicadas hummed forever and ever, a reminder they weren't alone, but there they were with all these thoughts and no one else so it got to them more than they liked to admit and they looked down the corridor of road for any light but none came. Everyone was in a bed, tight with a loved one or themselves, to fade. And there Orion was gyrating in the black road, willing someone to come so they could jump out of the way and be scared back to the real world. They

69

drifted into sleep for a couple hours but dawn was far away. Months and months. So they ran Sims but that only reminded them they were in a car trying to pass the time. A truck finally appeared in the distance. The reality of their situation became apparent and they hid. It wasn't until afternoon the next day they felt comfortable flagging someone down for a charge.

"Why didn't you call me?" I asked.

"This was last year," said Orion.

"Why didn't you call your partner then?" They sighed and looked off.


In the morning, Sci's beat-up Camry was parked across the street. They sipped from a thermos and rolled the window down at my approach. They figured it was easier to find me than find the job.

"So, where we going?" they asked.

"'I cannot disclose the claim nor its location out of adherence to the strictest confidentiality agreement between federal agency and citizen.'"

"Just get in your little raspberry." That's what they called my truck.

Our neighborhood kept its blues and greys. The sky was saturated as it shook off the night. When we broke out, gold flooded the fields, reflecting whatever it found. Empty silos choked under green veins, tilting this way or that. We sped around tourists whose self-drive hugged one side of the road. Gunning it between fields, running with the clouds.

A sandy brick building, five stories tall, and thirty minutes outside Spencer, had a tree in the lobby that we could see from the parking lot. Its branches shot out the windows on all sides like a boxy pinecone. It had housed a startup from St. Paul that had something to do with nutrient supplements. They went out of business eight months prior and abandoned that building a year into Overgrowth. There was a chain on the door loosened enough that we could squeeze in if we pushed hard.

Sci whistled and craned their neck up the atrium, following the tree. A dried-up fountain encircled the maple. I stepped into the ring and sat where the fewest beer cans, needles, and plastic bags were.

Dried dirt crusted under my feet. Creaking doors echoed around the atrium at Sci's inspection. Metal clanged onto concrete. *I'm ok!* I chuckled to myself. I focused on a leaf between the third and fourth floor, fluttering, split in the sun's rays.

Howard asked us to inspect abandoned buildings thoroughly to ensure no one submitted a claim again. I hollered a couple times to draw anyone out, but only Sci peaked into the center to see what was up.

The maple went straight, and only its branches swayed under a high breeze. I rested against the lip of the fountain and

71

put my chin to my chest.

It was night in our neighborhood, and I was running down the street. Someone was chasing me with a pipe to crack me over the head, and there was no one left in the houses to hear my screams, until Sci kicked me. The light slanted.

"Hey. How long was I out?"

"I don't know. Look what I found." They grabbed a clean OnBoard, two candles, and a calendar of very average-looking men. A gag gift that prompted an HR email, we imagined.

"You go to a lot of abandoned buildings in this line of work?" they asked.

"Just a barn, a McMansion, this place."

I told them about Wynne, about Yates and Grayson and Claire. They came unbidden, and I missed Yates. Sci looked off to a clump of desks. I was exhausted by the end and didn't want to answer the questions that were always coming from them.

"What happened to Grayson?" I didn't like thinking about them.

"Eh, nothing I imagine." I squirmed. "Probably still on their OnBoard."

"I know a couple kids from foster care. It was hard, but they're better than they would've been with their parents."

"Well, good for them."

"I'm not saying that's what you should've done. I'm just sharing."

"Yeah, yeah."

"Well I just think Lou Anne's being a bit of a cunt, that's all!"

"Sharon!"

"What? Am I wrong?"

"That's not nice."

"Oh to hell with that, I said what I said."

"It's a *book* club, Sharon."

"And bully for her. I am just as invested as you all are."

"Sim's not the same."

"Right, it's better. Wanna know how Gabriel's hands felt? Oh no, you'll just imagine it huh?"

And Sharon knew it wasn't about the book, it was just an excuse to meet every week, and who could be expected to finish a book a week anyways? But Lou Anne was uppity about the whole thing and wasn't showing up anymore out of spite.

A tabby burrowed under Ginny's arm, and she stroked them, listening to Sharon. A fat tuxedo flicked its tail against the flies. The other three were somewhere among the stacks. The Spencer Public Library always had at least one cat since Dewey Readmore Books: a kitten, abandoned in the drop box back in the eighties and taken in by the staff. Ginny kept the two-foot statue of Dewey free of vines and weeds, a sandy smile among the green. The library was better kept than most places — books didn't take well to sunlight — so the inside was frozen, a collection of all knowledge up until just before Overgrowth, that is until the ceiling collapsed or the foundation burst. It was the only place solitude felt full.

I could tell Sharon was trying to make me laugh, so I resisted, which only made it harder, until I did crack a smile and she pointed, *See! They know what I'm talking about!* and they invited me over. She laid into Lou Anne enough that I could feel the endearment, as potent as Ginny's in her patience. I shared how I didn't read but that Mom stopped checking out sims based on books a while back, how she liked her choices more. Sharon respected that but couldn't get off as easily with one hand. Ginny held her head in her hands, shook it back and forth, giddy. It was strange. I remembered details now to relay them back to Sci, imagining their reaction.

When Ginny took me through the stacks I was fascinated by how unassuming it felt. I had read before, a long time ago, and knew how much information was packed into each tome. The words should have mauled me, overpowered me with their worlds and lobotomies. But they rested. And if I picked one up it did nothing to compel me. Only the weight and that smell. The categories were broader — Sci-fi, Romance, Fantasy, Literature, Non-Fiction, Religion — which is probably why they died out.

74

When I picked a sim I knew the experience I was getting. Though I suppose I liked the ones that subverted my expectations the most. The investment killed books then. I opened a red spine in front of me and there was no hook. *Eventually* I would care. But I might not. Why wait around? Ginny seemed to sense this because she asked me what I liked to do and I shrugged. Same stuff as anyone I supposed — walking, talking, eating. Soft light in the eyes. She came back with a classic-looking thing — a cover of a bunch of people standing around.

"What's it about?"

"Absolutely nothing." *A Tale of Two Cities.*

I thought Cicadas would be louder out there. Instead they were everywhere. This pervasive, electric tune. These crescendos from nowhere; so much I still couldn't see. If I forgot about it I might feel it for a moment, and I felt like a kid, *Did you see what I did?* Which meant I should walk on and leave it be. Hoped there was space for someone else.

The house was overrun by ferns. These wide, double Windows were to blame, and a homeowner who couldn't imagine a dark house. At least the solar-powered weedwhacker was ready.

"Your OnBoard works better in the dark anyways," I

said.

"Oh I never bought into those," said Henry. "My phone works just fine."

"Ok. Can you show me the before photos?" And he clicked and clicked, tapped, tapped, tapped, and clicked, and *oh, that's not it.*

I crawled along the ground to find the roots and ripped, ripped. Sci flitted through their notes.

We played this game where I'd start describing something in the room and Sci would have to guess what it was.

"A chip on its shoulder. Like a beach."

"What the fuck does that mean."

"I don't know, figure it out."

"Ok, ok." And they moved me a little, stood where I stood. "I need perspective." Their eyes went elsewhere, and I wondered why. Until they saw it and beamed. Yes, the tile. They got better at it like that. Seeing where I reached.

"It's like every job's worse," I said.

"Entropy."

"Huh?"

"Entropy: things get more chaotic."

"Thought it was decay."

And they huffed, stood, because it was all so simple really. "Entropy is the heat, or energy, lost in any closed system operation."

"So like burning charge in a car."

"No. That charge goes toward the engine. But entropy is the charge that's lost to the process — feeding it through the cable and motor and lights. The exact output doesn't match the charge."

"Oh, sure."

They shifted back and forth. A vine hung by their face and they ripped it down.

"So how does that apply here?" I asked.

"Well. The second law of thermodynamics dictates that entropy, the loss of heat in a closed system, is always increasing."

"So?"

"The more concentrated an action, the more chaotic the byproduct. And if the universe is a closed system, from the big bang on, ever-expanding, then things are gradually more chaotic, until all heat has reached equilibrium."

"Like I'm five."

"Your coffee eventually becomes the same temperature as the room. The heat didn't go anywhere, just dispersed through the room, expanded to where you can't feel it. But to make the coffee you had to boil the pot. So contraction predicates an expansion."

"And the plants are the coffee?" We went over it a few more times.

Sci liked explaining things to me as I *don't know much and*

77

*don't argue* and throughout the day pinged files to my OnBoard on whatever the lecture was. Physics, zoology, engineering. They kept to the concepts, knowing math would only spoil things. Still enough to make my head swim.

"What are you doing?" they asked. I was bent at the waist.

"Stretching." Left to right, right to left. Chest to the sky.

"Who taught you that?"

"Danny. My brother." I hadn't thought about it.

"You look pliant." An odd look.

They were from Indiana and wouldn't go back. Their family was still there but they liked the idea of settling their own spot and having somewhere for the rest of them to see; after grad school they'd end up at a university or lab. They laughed when I called them a bad teacher. They knew they loved it and thought about centering their life around academia. *You ask more circular questions though.* The only commonality would be not much money which neither of us really cared about so it wasn't much of a discussion.

"We're from South Carolina, actually," said Blake. He'd made lemonade that tasted like tea. All the water out there tasted like dirt. There was probably something in the pipes, clinging to the water as it passed through. But every town insisted that it was clean and healthy, so what's the point in arguing. Water flowed, and that was more than I had expected.

"When did you move out here?" I asked.

"Oh, couple years ago? Time's funny nowadays, yea?"

"Yeah. But after Overgrowth?"

"Well that's the whole reason we came!"

"Ok."

"You ever hear that one?"

"Can't say I have."

"Right, 'cause the media's scared them all shitless of the greatest miracle the world's ever seen."

"I've heard that."

"Yeah, from preservationists — and I'm happy for it — but that's not why. Breathe in." I did. "Longer." I let the first out, then sucked from my gut. "Full circle." He took one too.

I felt light-headed, squatted slightly so my fingers grazed the grass. They got along with the moisture in the air, or that was the theory. Some protection against droughts if you subscribed to the ag science origin. Whatever they pumped out seemed juiced, like I was sticking my head in an old freezer — pure oxygen, stuff you might get high off of.

"Imagine growing up on it," he said. "Jonah and Mitchy are gonna be tall as pines. Just think what the food's doing for us."

"Couple super kids."

"Hahaha, that's right! Just wish I was their age. Did fix

79

my knee though. Used to spend all day just lying around, hurt so bad. Now look at me!" He did a small jig, buckled halfway through.

We went to a fair in a field bent by autumn floods. A couple families milled around the Ferris wheel and giant slide. One guy in a blue jumpsuit reading "Kurt's Thrill Stop" walked around all day with a pack of weedkiller around his waist, pumping it onto the rides in a flurry of mist. A couple teenagers stood at the end of the game booth aisles and ran into whichever game someone wanted to play until the customer got tired or cheated and the teenager joined up with their buddy in a sim.

"Why are you guys here anyways?" I asked after spraying my bumblebee forward.

"Eh, not sure about here," she said. "But lots of towns have these kinds of things every year, get real sentimental about it. It's an easier gig if you ask me."

Clouds gathered overhead, the scent of rain. Dew formed on our foreheads. I felt winded. Yellow umbrellas flapped, threatening to take off. Weedkiller droplets flew over and stung my eyes. The siren started as we were about to step onto the tilt-a-whirl. We ran to the rental truck, figuring it was heavier than Sci's sedan. The grey darkened to black streaks as we heard the wind whistle around the car. A loop rollercoaster strained against its wiring then fell, enveloped in the prairie grass that shivered this way then that, and I thought the whole thing might lift into the sky and spin around the funnel like a ring. It was far off, an insect leg pressing clouds into the dirt. It was in our neighborhood's direction, and I worried about Orion. Coverage was out, and I cursed the satellites. Of course Orion was fine, but the unknown of it all was unnecessary.

I smoked Sci up for the first time. "You know what it's doing to our brains, right?" they said. And of course I knew, I knew every other night, but pretended not to so they could explain and that was love in a way I had forgotten and they must have felt it because it reached across the center console and threatened to crush the whole thing.

Orion and I connected when it passed. They were in the car when the siren sounded then gunned it away from the funnel in the sky. On a highway just outside of town they parked the car over the median and sat on the hood to watch it spiral.

Denise Perkins was dead along with half a dozen other folks.

*Superposition* Sci had called it. The idea that something was and wasn't. *Totally overshadowed by the nuke* but informed everything we did since. Schrodinger's Cat was more than a cat in a box, dead and alive; no, it was our plaything. The cat only ever existed because we considered it, dreamt it up, and its fate was the same. Our observation was a decision. Because superposition meant that we could never truly observe the location of atoms. The moment energy is measured, position has changed, and vice versus. That's how I came to understand Orion's marriage.

If I asked about Jordan, Orion might huff, *Who knows what they're doing.* Or they looked out the window and imagined where they might be. They hummed a sweet song while putting away the dishes, then made a crack about how Jordan never cleaned out a glass, always left it "for later" but grabbed a fresh one next time. They laughed at an incoming message, shook their head, *I hate them.* But more than anything, Orion didn't want to think about it too much. Observation would mean a decision, so better to leave it in the box and wonder or dread what might be happening inside.

A crash woke me up. I didn't think about it again until the next morning. The elm had grown through the loop I hung the weedwhacker on and slipped it off the hook, dropping it to the ground, breaking only the solar panel.

Spencer yielded to whatever was present — fields shaped for crops or grass or developments — and was eternal for it. The homes might decay and lose themselves to vines, but it was a crust of land, one scratch away from what was before, layered and layered.

Sci scoffed when someone called it the Great Lakes region. Not The Great Lakes — The Iowa Great Lakes. There were a few big lakes just north of Spencer where people got away for the summers and weekends.

"You can't see the other side of Lake Michigan!" said Sci.

"Sure."

"That's a *Great* Lake. Like five states are solely based around their existence."

We went up one weekend and got jet skis, skimmed the space between us so we rocked in the wake. When our time was up we laid on the beach under an umbrella and dried off. No blanket or anything so the sand shaped to us. It was all artificial but cradled nonetheless. I started the book Ginny gave me and recognized the opening. *Best and worst.* I watched Sci, still on their side. When had I last seen someone else's goosebumps?

"It's like when the rain's stopped and the sun's setting," said Sci. A variant of our game.

"Tranquil."

"Close, but you can smell the rain still and it feels more like morning. It's like that opposite time of what time it is, but it feels good."

"I get what you're saying but I don't think there's a word for that."

"No there is. We just can't think of it."

"But I get what you're saying."

"Not really." They chewed their lip. Their OnBoard flickered fast, eyes darted. And the day unraveled around us. Because even by the time Sci gave up there was an unease in the air, a humming in their head, scratching but they didn't even know it. I sat back, turned my mind forward to the night and it's black, its dawn, its wheel. And it spun fast, faster until I was humming, and I wished I could hold Sci but they were trying to keep their head above water, didn't realize they were flailing. Oh, what a pair. A breeze blew and we were freezing. How could we think we wouldn't need blankets? And Sci did some jumping jacks to get warm, kicked at me, stopping their foot just short, and I grabbed it and flipped it up. They howled and tilted back, grabbed my arms and pulled me down, conking our heads together. An icy pain spread from my crown, but we were laughing.

I was out at Lucy's Roadside with a lager when a weight clapped down on my right shoulder and I jumped away into the next stool. A guy in cargo shorts wanted to know where I was from. So I told him, and he had a buddy from Philly whose house he was going to, so I should come along and I did. It was a standard affair of four in a yard, kicking rocks, with enough beer for any sucker they brought in. A fly zapper popped blue over the porch entrance as they took turns kicking burning logs from the bonfire, showering sparks across the circle, making flashes of the person opposite.

Two of them were squatting in the place. Layla's dad was a sheriff in Minnesota so she figured the natural thing to do was run away, and Nick got a girl pregnant in Mississippi. Together with cargo short Trevor and lanky Craig, they'd make it out West. Trevor had hoped I was another stray with cash, which I was but wasn't. A buddy back east received most of my paycheck for investment, so I was liquid in only the ways that mattered. Craig fed me beers.

The last flaming log flew over the moon and we retired to squatting. Such towns were rich in raw material: industrial floodlights, tarpaulin, road signs, dirty mattresses, booze. Nick produced a torch lighter and burned space to sit until Craig shoved him for trying to burn the place down. Layla slipped out.

"Porn sim," said Trevor. "Won't go an hour without it, the freak. Bet she got thrown out when they caught her."

Nick brought out Red and passed it around. I considered it but didn't want Sci seeing me the next morning all despondent. The boys burned and pumped their fists. I lit a joint.

"See, see," said Craig.

"Yeah!"

"This. This is what it is."

"Yeah man."

"And in Oregon, we'll do it our way."

"Yeah man. West baby."

"No, no," I said. "They did that, they did that. It's just a place to go."

"Exactly!"

"No! You keep going till you drop, and when you drop all you think is you wish you can go but you can't."

"That's right bud, burn it out, blow it out."

"For what? You just go and go for nothing." Trevor kicked holes in the wall in rhythmic *duhn, duhn, duhn*s. Nick got in my face.

"Who's this, Trevor? Real sag." I stayed placid until he got bored. I sat back. Craig whooped and hollered in the corner, exuberant over the revelations. Peaceful after I removed myself. Then I could see the burn out, *collapsing possibilities*. I wished them luck heading west and left. The truck got me back late. A message came in as I crossed the threshold.

*Out of town, bck by wknd*

Orion came back Saturday afternoon. "I have to take care of some things. I'm picking up some claims along the way. Howard's aware." And they were out before the end of the hour.

We were clearing a duplex near the highway when Sci started complaining about the food. I never understood this, because Dropped food out there was the same as Dropped food back home, which they couldn't believe — couldn't believe I Dropped food when I had access to a kitchen. So when I told them I had a kitchen, yes a functioning kitchen, currently, they were furious I hadn't told them sooner and demanded we cook that night. But I didn't have anything, so we would have to go grocery shopping too, and when we were there I got self-conscious that I didn't know how to make most of the dishes they listed, which didn't make any sense because they knew everything that I didn't but I couldn't take this, so I nodded and let myself get caught up in their excitement of the dishes that sprang to mind and we were riding the shopping cart until I flipped and turned beet red while they cackled like I had never heard, so I almost intentionally slipped on the way up and the thought alone must have pushed me because then I really did, hitting the ground hard on my forearms and it sounded like they were choking, gasping for breath. *Stop! I'm gonna pee!*

Three grocery bags sat in the passenger seat of my truck with the seat belt over them because they were the most precious things I had hauled in a long time. We had enough for leftovers and dessert. I dreaded how long it would all take, but then I remembered I had not one thing better to do. Sci was behind me, flicked their brights, bumped up against me at red lights. I pinged them, *gnna run me off the road.*

The kitchen windows were still taped up because Orion and I didn't hang out in there much. The pale red flowers looked purple in the lamplight.

"I bet the slope out front helped the house stay relatively clear," said Sci. "No water to pool and fester."

"I was going to say the exact same thing." I brought out every bowl and pan we had. "So do we start by pissing on it or jumping up and down on it?"

"'Oh I'm from the East Coast! I won't eat anything less than medium rare.'" They pushed their nose up like a pig.

"Do you eat steak medium well out here?"

"Do you hear yourself? It's breadcrumbs and gravy, you'll live."

I beat the cube steaks between plastic while Sci mixed baking soda, powder, pepper, salt, then buttermilk, hot sauce, and eggs. I coated the steaks in flour while Sci heated the shortening to 325 degrees, then I dipped them in the batter, back in the flour, into the skillet to pop. Just a couple minutes, each side.

Gravy was easier than I thought. The fat from the pan, the solid bits from the bottom, with some milk until thick.

And I wanted to maul something the smell bit so. But we needed to make cookies.

"Dough feels like cheating," I said. They shrugged.

"Why you add caramel."

So they baked while we ate twice as much as we had intended to, and when Orion came in we were laughing because we had finished the wine.

"Didn't know we had company," said Orion.

"Right," I said. "Orion, this is Sci — Sci, Orion." They

nodded then looked over the food. "Do you want some? We have plenty of leftovers. Cookies are in the oven."

"Not hungry." They said this on the way out.

Sci pinged, *shame*.

We wrapped the cookies in paper towels for the tour. The caramel made a difference. Our hands lingered along the walls, following a current to my room. It felt like a place then, more than a sleeping area. Where one might go to get away.

Sci stumbled from the bedframe to the window, opened it, and hung out. They hollered farther and farther until a knee was out into that empty town, and I thought they'd fall and grabbed them by the waist. Familiar. They laughed as we fell onto the seat in front of the bay.

"Who's this?" They held up a handful of leaves.

"Gary Jr.," I said.

"Cute."

"Thought Midwesterners could handle their liquor."

"Oh you bet — I can go all night." And they burst in a fit of laughs, holding their face by their knees. They sighed. We chewed on the cookies. "Was just trying to keep up with you."


A week later we finished initial claims and started following up on unanswered ones. Sci joined me for a few of these but was busy when I went back to the nutrient startup with the tree in the center. I called out to the atrium in a decrescendo

89

and found my spot at the outside of the fountain ring and sat back. I thought about Overbrook, getting more houseplants, but remembered they would need more attendance back there. Gary Jr. had a few inches of dirt but yards of leaves trailing from the old pesto jar. The urge to toss it into the woods and forget about it rather than kill it in some apartment. I put my chin to my chest and dreamt. The slit was gone but I kept picking at where it was because I could still feel it surging beneath the skin, sliding up my forearm, jerking my shoulder to reach for something I couldn't see but it knew was there. *Move, damnit.* If I broke through the surface would it pour out and let me sleep? I woke up, the red still below my wrist.

Orion drove us out. Sci sent a photo of the loop rollercoaster, or where it was. Grass ensnared the blue mess of metal and wires so only a circular hump was visible. Sci said Kurt's Thrill Stop called it quits and was banking on insurance money after the tornado. They sold what they could, which wasn't much, leaving verdant obtrusions that would lose feature soon. I imagined the teenagers hooking up with Trevor and the rest of them to make it west. We shambled along.

Redfield, South Dakota proved the world got flatter and sparser the less I knew about it. We were stopped by a construction crew working a busted bridge at the northern tip of town; the banks beside it were charred, with green dots creeping, threatening to swallow the crane. A team of five with propane tanks on their backs swept the area. After the first pass they torched it again and a bit more of the edge. They wore worn, mustard firefighter gear, patched at the elbows and sleeves. Orion said they were a bunch of nuts.

There were no rentals in the area, so Orion dropped me off in the middle of 6th Avenue. Some claims were on the edge of town, miles down the road, so I figured I'd start there and work in. The way out was a straight shot of grassy banks, relaxed against the sky, content in their short reach. A house took shape, white, like a kid might draw. It was the first time someone pulled a gun on me. The barrel was as big as my head, dead-on and cat-black.

"Is this the Steelman residence?" I asked.

"Why?"

"You submitted an Overgrowth claim, and I'm following up on it."

"That was in the fall."

"We're following up on it."

"I don't want your type around," she said. "I'm gonna keep this on you until I can't see you. Now get!" I kept my hands up and walked backwards before flipping at the end of the driveway.

There was another claim half a mile down but I thought

91

it best to move toward town. The new June sun cooked me while I kicked it back. A speck of the house was on the horizon half an hour later. A shot rang out while I stood staring at it. I hustled, crouched, waving in the direction 6th Avenue. The grass reached over, tunneling along. I dared to stand when I heard a car coming, started jogging, refused to turn around. She was running me down, one hand on the wheel, the other hanging the shotgun out the window. It was a dead heat, my arms pumping. A green pickup sailed past. Momentum threw me a few paces while the truck stopped ahead. I stared for a bit until they reversed.

"You trying to race?" they said.

"No," I said. "Thought you were running me down." They laughed. I explained the situation.

"Mm. Yeah, Jeanie's been in a mood these past few months," they said. "One of her cats got out and she thinks we kept it. I'm Cleo, they/he." They wore a rag of a button down a few sizes too big and leaned back while they drove. Cleo invited me for a smoke back at their place. *Can't imagine the stress you just took on.* It was this old farmhouse with two dozen rooms and half as many cars parked around the circle drive. Their room was in the east wing, tucked into an attic they had done up with floating lights and soundproofing. I rolled a spliff from what Cleo had and a couple cigarettes in my back pocket. No one from that residence had ever submitted a claim.

"You work?" I asked.

"Oh yeah," Cleo exhaled. "Tech, you know."

"Ah yeah, good gig."

"Mhm, pays the bills. Working right now." We laughed. So was I.

This couple, Yuri and Jenna, bought the place just before Overgrowth, which even then cost nothing. They knew plenty of wanderers to bring out and build a community. So it grew, and shrank, and plenty cleared out after Overgrowth, but it always had some free corner, which Cleo seized after a falling out with an ex in Kansas City. Yuri left for Nevada a few years back but Jenna stayed and probably would until she passed, to everyone's delight, because Jenna mowed the lawn and didn't ask for much in rent. Cleo had an idea of who Orion was, but Simon was the real scribe, so we went looking for him in the workshop on the west side of the place.

The halls were packed with right angles: paintings, portraits, and maps, many signed with a left slanting scribble. Cleo said it was Gaia's mark, which they wouldn't elaborate on, *they're Gaia's mark, dude.* A wail floated, operatic, *Moss, in the garden.* A few people wondered if I was a stray.

"No, we're just high," said Cleo.

Simon was using a power saw when we came in and pointed to safety goggles by the door without looking up. His station had tidy piles of wood around the perimeter, sectioning it off from the scrap metal, canvases, and wires around the rest of the workshop. We sat in two unstained chairs while he finished slicing; the pieces falling in hollow plunks until he had the parts for a table.

"What brings you around, Clinker?"

"That Dick, son!" Cleo chuckled and introduced us. Simon's hand felt like a mannequin's, bent for so long into a couple shapes, calloused.

"You know Orion," I said.

"That I do," said Simon. "Must have been last year? Year before?"

"Probably."

"You're part of the NOER team then?"

"Yes. Just seeing if you all need anything."

"Jeanie Evans tried to shoot them!" said Cleo. Simon sighed and shook his head.

"Damn. She still think we took the cat?"

"Well we killed it."

"Don't say that, no we didn't." He turned to me. "Someone hit it, and we buried it."

"Why not tell her?" I asked.

"Oh, they hate us here," said Cleo.

"They don't hate us. But no, it doesn't look great, and it was already lost and probably going to die some other way," said Simon.

"And they don't hate you all."

"Right. Just not used to us."

"Uh huh," said Cleo. "And they wanna fuck us. It's confusing."

The Peanut crew stopped by Redfield. Three kids just out of college, piloting this giant nut across the country. It was inevitable I saw it again, like a Georgian mirage. Orion and I first ran into them in Wynne, then again driving up to Spencer. Outsiders like Orion, Sci, and myself were pulled into each other's orbit, colliding out there.

Kari was driving, draped over the wheel, and I flagged them down. They had heard about the tornado in Spencer and were glad to hear we were all right.

"Where's Orion?" asked Dale.

"I don't know, on a job."

"Yeah, they're not attached at the hip," said Kari. "Not like we hang out all the time."

"Uh, yeah," said Jake. "We kind of do."

"Maybe you guys," said Kari.

"You hit us up for drinks last night," said Jake.

"Ok, you know what I'm saying."

"Think she's embarrassed by us, bud," said Dale.

"Oh, fuck off." She pushed him. Dale laughed.

They let me drive the truck. It handled easier than I'd guessed, except when the wind got bad over a plain and it nudged

95

us near a ditch. It was strange seeing everyone turn to look. That porous monstrosity. The horn wasn't anything special. They had more rules than not letting anyone else drive it: no bars, liquor stores, anything that could become a meme. It sounded exhausting and less freeing than it should be. They dropped me off at the next job with a few bags of cinnamon-dusted nuts.

The Blaze Team met at Freeman's every night, spent. They sought me out when they heard we were in town and wanted to know what other Overgrowth sites were like. I described them as like Redfield, but they didn't think anywhere was like Redfield because they had the Blaze Team, which was twenty or so men with propane on their backs, burning fields. They wanted to get deputized by the governor and thought I could help. I told them I only knew Howard, but they knew bureaucracy was an intricate web of favors and insisted I call one in, so I told them I'd think about it, and they bought me three rounds. Every day they got up and needed to take back more of their home, through soot and burns and tears.

I borrowed Orion's car one Saturday morning because the air was cool and fresh. So much ground to cover. To the east was a river that wound down before getting lost in a creek. Ratty fields looped, broken by tree lines. I blew through one town after the next. One looked deserted, but I felt eyes on my foreign car, and I wondered who else saw Overgrowth as an opportunity.

I told myself again and again I wasn't looking for anything, and I didn't find anything. I punched it down the center of the road until I thought I'd hit an invisible wall and flip. I set a route hours away and switched off. Slants of sunlight blessed spots ahead, and I hoped to drive through one.

I came to in the orange of summer on the side of the road. Three hours from town, and Orion had pinged me a dozen times, which bugged me — it was my day off. A burger was what I needed, so I input "Redfield" and kept my head on a swivel.

We were holed up in a motel again, but I spent most of my time at The Ranch on Cleo's floor. I'd finish a claim and have them pick me up to get out into the fields or thickets or ponds, wild and hollering the whole way. Cleo would start talking to themselves, picking fights with ghosts or spilling their cranium all over the dash while I caved in on myself, through the window out onto the fields, a different solidarity. Then we'd get home. This gal, Germaine, lived in the east wing, in a long room turned nebular with its watercolor walls, where she burned coals for hookah on a hot plate that fell and ate through the rugs. Jenna didn't want any hard drugs in the house so we mixed and matched because limitations breed creativity and there were a dozen of us geeked out, floating, pawing at each other for kicks and I figured I found it again after so long but couldn't understand why it all had to be segmented like that with Sci in Nebraska and my friends all gone. One night we were out on the raft in the pond behind the main house when Germaine's roommate did a back flip and came up screaming about being dragged, that the plants were growing onto them and I said that science made it so and everyone laughed and I figured I found it again but it was like running a race that was over.

The Ranch dealt with Overgrowth well because every part moved, even in the quiet ways of Len and Hugo who painted and read with a ferocity I felt two rooms over. A gaggle of creatives, engineers, runaways, story-book characters.

I started losing things. Nothing I cared about, but they slipped like water in flight, and I knew it was a beautiful time.

They put me in their group chat and I wanted to scream.

Kris and Wells kept coming up. Everyone asked when they might be back or what they were up to, which Cleo didn't know. Last he heard the two were in Chicago for some new rendezvous.

I was trying to fall asleep when I thought about Sci, not the parts that were real, but all that could've been. I needed to pass out, to be hit over the head, but it all came unbidden — calls and visits and meeting friends, meeting family. I could hear the tone they would use with Danny. Particle by particle I obliterated us. Orion was right — hope shot right through it. I couldn't just leave us alone so that it might endure; no, I had to wring it out, watch it dissolve at my feet.

Cleo and I heard of a woman who could perform a death ritual. Cleo insisted we should learn what it was like before it came and I had nothing better to do than follow them around. Germaine caught wind and convinced Simone to come as well.

The shaman's place was set back from the road through a forest floor that smelled of cardamom. Only the glass reflecting on the door hinted at a home. Inside, the front rooms were cleaned of anything human to give the impression of a fairy site, a green box plucked from the Earth. Her name was Jody, and she had witnessed 24 deaths, prompted three of them.

"Do we have to get naked?" asked Cleo.

She shrugged. "Most are clothed when they go. You do you."

Jody explained she would prompt a kind of psychosis, and where we landed was for us to decide. She closed the blinds, instructed us to lie down in the grass, touch our hip, then stomach, then chest, then throat.

"Your body is not your mind, feel how it sinks. Look straight ahead, up — this is how we've always gone." She left us in silence as I felt my head clear out. "This is your greatest illusion to overcome. This tie to a you. Let it go." River was out again with the Ranch, probably drinking. "The unity you crave is on the other side of acceptance. Let go." And if Claire could just accept this, we could be a family again, a real one dammit. "Give up this invention, this refraction." Simon almost slipped but for his tie to Wells. The four fell into dreamless sleep.

When we were kids Danny and I used to climb on top of the playground equipment. And Mom yelled at us but gave up once we were seven and nine because by then we were all limbs and could grab onto anything, and if we fell and broke our necks that'd make sure the other never did it again. We'd bury each other with woodchips and mourn, but then we'd move on because the playground was still there.

Danny taught me to smoke in the tube slide — thirteen and fifteen. We were scared someone would smell the smoke, so we thought the tube would cover some of it. I pressed my feet against the grey top to keep from sliding down. It was yellow during the day and one hundred and ten degrees, and it was still stuffy that night but a breeze came through sometimes. He lit the roll and I could see his face, orange spreading from the tip of his crooked nose. *Watch, watch.* An inhale, hold, inhale, pointing down to his lungs, circling up through his chest to his head, out his nose. I tried but kept blowing it out too soon. Tasted like grass which was funny. And maybe I was high, but I doubt it. We laughed a lot in the tube though.

*Keep to the real shit, if you're gonna at all.*

~

Day burns made the most logistical sense, so the Blaze Team could see how much they were taking out, how much was left. Night burns were better in the symbolic sense. I got invited to one on a Sunday after we had drunken beers at Jose's all noon, afternoon, evening; god summer stretched. It finally got dark and they donned their fireman gear first — the rags — before setting the propane on the picnic tables, hefting them. I had no intention of joining them until the seventh beer. Then I learned the focus they maintained, each heavy step in conversation with the terrain. Jerry puffed a flame at me and I stumbled onto my back like a turtle, inept, the guys laughing, until they helped me up and I puffed him back before Charlie stepped in and led us out, stalking the streets; the pavement holy road in its surety. The fear of Orion or Cleo recognizing me plucked through. I sunk into the anonymity of the masks.

The west side of town had been an issue forever. The river ran there and before Overgrowth it flooded and sank the grain mill, and now the green burst from its banks so that it was downright offensive. The Blaze Team went out there every Sunday because there was always more. We spread into a police line thirty feet apart a piece so I couldn't see either end. Some had run in and were waiting for the call: a pop in the dark. Charlie started.

"WE BLAZE."

101

"WE BURN."

"THE FIGHT?"

"IN TURN."

"TO REST?"

"TO DIE."

"RAISE IT HIGH."

And the light filled my goggles before I felt myself pulling the trigger. I tucked the flamethrower to my ribs and oscillated, stomping the cinders, forward, toward the team that had gone ahead and went up in bonfires. The mask only blocked so much heat before seeping through; but I was beyond my face, simply hands that continued their task without eyes that clouded or skin that seared. Like cutting onions, tears streaming down, felt but ignored. Clean, clean, it went underfoot. So simple. And I lost track of the team so when the yellow solidified and ran into me we were mad and hugging each other in the flames, then breaking down our paths into the center, the red, yanking dead matter in our hands just to burn it up close. Sweltering in the suit. Sweat or the heat. Run and kick the log to sparks.

We were losing steam, propane, so Jerry ran further in and shot all around, at the branches, so embers rained, and we ran at him and followed his lead, then torched him with the last of what we had so he was screaming before running out of the circle a burning man. What an idiot.

"The bank's beautiful," said Charlie. "Takes a new shape

every time we blaze, each more lovely than the last. And I'm glad we're the only ones who see it, that we can crumble it before anyone else does. I hope it gets to where we can't burn without the vines smashing our heads together, and it just keeps going until it takes the town, and no one comes back."

Jose and Kevin got in a fight over the clock again. They always did, and we let them go at it for a while before it got physical, then we circled, voicing some caution. *Man, he's not worth it.* Kevin knew the Main Street clock should go, preserved, taken away before something took it; Jose knew it was as good as ripping out the heart, that if it went we'd all be stuck here in the same moment forever. Jose jumped on Kevin, staining his yellow rags with blood. We let it go a while before Charlie got him off, because we all knew Jose was right, but we wouldn't leave Kevin for the weeds. Our hoods were down in the bonfire air on the sure ground of heaven, back to Jose's for walk-me-downs.

I passed out on the lawn with the three in the Blaze Team who weren't married. I got up at dusk, in the mist, stumbled back to the house for a couple hours rest before the first claim.


I got separated from Cleo while roaming the property. Paths thread in curves through the woods and crisscrossed, so some loop would take you away and another brought you back and another ate you whole. I heard her singing first and followed it. Bertie's hut grew out of a hollow, in which she had her bed and main chest. Interlocking roots and ivy made up the dome that started at the lip of the hill and touched down some twenty feet from her bed. Inside she had woven eucalyptus and mint into the walls to keep out bugs. The floor was dirt, beaten, and she asked me to stamp a few sections as she didn't wear shoes. Her goal was to train the elm on the hill to take root around the dome by next summer, the dome then being guided by chicken wire in the spring.

"What about the winter?" I asked. "Does it stick around?"

The wind caught her laugh. "No, things still die. I move back to the main house around November. It's not really pleasant until May."

Bertie dated a friend of Jenna's decades ago, when they were both in Cleveland and kept in touch. Bertie was the first to move in, acting as the de facto matriarch.

"Must be a pain. Getting it growing every time," I said. She shrugged.

"Feels good to wake it back up. Reminds me it'll all start again."

She floated out there, letting her fingertips wander the dripping green. Then she was darting, hand and foot forward over an errant root until she caught the momentum in a lolling step and kept going, giggling, fluid.

We visited quiet corners of the property. Ancient trees

formed the perimeter like centurions protecting the mushy interior — permitting violet wildflowers to forget a vicious world.

"We're really into crickets lately."

"Crickets?"

"Yeah, we were blazing one night couple months ago while this one kept humming and humming — drove Charlie crazy. He threw off the pack and crept around for it. By the time we finished he was still working through the fields, then we're all searching and we're out till Martha's calling me and I tell her 'Babe, it's a mythic cricket," so they're laughing, and now we're always on the hunt for one — the mythic cricket."

"That's cute."

He laughed. They went on burning. Afterward I asked Charlie about the crickets and he told me how they've been harbingers of destruction forever, in every culture, that it could signal locusts. I said that a swarm might help them, and he looked off, *No, no that's different.* The festering.

I dreamt. I was in a field with Orion and Yates. We were arguing over whether we could go back into town or not: vampires had overrun the place. Orion wanted to check for survivors while Yates wanted to set a basecamp. I didn't want to go but let them argue. I remembered the chase through the woods and my blood pumping, yelling at the two of them to take this path or that — felt like I had walked for a reason. I couldn't remember why they stopped chasing us, and that must have summoned them because they were behind us and jumping and I woke up in a sweat.

Some mornings I woke up and forgot where I was. Others I woke up and thought I hadn't slept — a blink between the last and first light. Or I shook off the dream, looked around the room for continuity. My yellow backpack was the best reference. Then I could get up and navigate the rest of the space.

Whatever had been intended for me before the job, I was far off course. Like a rudder tilted slightly, over eight months I'd land somewhere else. Where I could've been was distant, blurred.


I met Wells while Cleo helped him make cheesecake. His fingers were quick, pulling shakers and mixers just out of his grasp, cutting a frame or two. He thought baking too restrictive; though rewarding in its own right for its precision, and the intoxication it produced. Kris loved him in an apron too. His eyes made me squirm because they were rich and brown and soaked up too much at once, like his breath could take some of yours and give it back, new. I laughed and laughed and felt too smiley. He seemed to sense this and asked me to find Kris in the garden. He wanted her to taste test.

I knew Kris right away by how she glowed, and I wanted

to laugh all over again. She bent over squash, holding them in one hand while the other snapped shears. The words fell through me.

"Hi Kris."

"Oh, hi."

"Wells needs you in the kitchen."

"Oh does he now." She had already slipped behind me, tossed the shears and floppy hat into a neat pile. She waited in the doorway to the kitchen. I thought I'd fall into her from ten feet away how she pulled. "Oh my god, look at him!" said Kris. "Just want to jump him sometimes, you know?" I did. He could tell we were watching and made a face that Kris rushed, twirled his locks. Cleo thought they did it for show so much that they forgot and it became real.

They had been alone together for a while and expected they would for the latter half of their lives. But their favorite game lately was with Simon, sometimes engaging the whole house. He'd pull some trick that got Kris away: a new table he finished, a wine she'd love, that one time at the mask party, etc., slipping further and further until they were lost in the west wing. Or she would play the harlot, the spurned, and Simon the Sullen. It was a dance, playing off whatever mood the three were in. Once, Wells was so absorbed in his work he forgot to check on them all weekend. *It's honestly convenient when I'm trying to get shit done.* For her birthday, he'd affect Atlas and take them both in a fury, resolute and burning.

Any time I wasn't at the Ranch or on a job I was under a microscope, out there on the plains in my singularity, forever and ever. I had found it again and was desperate not to lose it, which I knew made me all the more likely to lose it, destined to lose and blow through town, just like I wanted. I'd find it again, I reasoned, find it over and over in every corner of the country so I could never be anywhere without it.

Once, I had this anxiety and Mom thought I should talk to someone about it. It was the usual stuff for teens: death, love, microplastics. We met once a week after school on Tuesdays and it felt like a big scam because they never taught me to get over it, only that I couldn't do anything about it. Amounted to "don't think about it so much" which was what I'd been trying to do, but there I was talking to someone about it.

I watched a bush burn for a while and I thought about the first plant I'd ever had. School had sent us home with these little pothoses right before the COVID pandemic. It sat in the window of me and Danny's room, growing a leaf then another in the spring sun. But Danny and I figured out how to fake being on camera in class while playing Fortnite and that was that. Mom was always at the hospital those days so we went to sleep with the lobby screen open and woke up just to turn it back on, to keep the music going. I watched the pothos brown, just a little on the edge at first, but it got worse, shriveling and turning stale so that I tried not to look at it, tried not to look out the window, because I knew I could've saved it any time, but it always felt too late. Must have been summer that things got a bit better because Mom was home more, and when she complained that all we did was sit around we barked back that that's all we did in school and I think she saw what had happened because she threw open every window and stripped our beds and almost threw out the pothos until I cried to leave it alone. *It's dead.* But I wouldn't hear it and screamed and screamed until she put it back down and I poured water on it until it dripped down the sill. The brown just killed me. And whenever Danny got mad at me he threatened to pluck off one of the dead leaves. When that first speck of green came back I jumped on Mom's bed until she got up and ran her over to it. It was alive, it was always alive. And the way it came back was a lot like how it died, in reverse, and I thought of Sci and entropy and it all blowing out just to snap back. The bush burning was disintegration. Blackened. Nothing left to grow from. But I knew even that wasn't true, I'd seen how untrue that was, how frustrating ashes were to the Blaze Team. Every bit left was fertilizer. Sometimes they'd even burn the ashes, scattering them farther, and I thought of the bits getting in our lungs and growing, vines crawling up the throat.

~

A reverie overcame the east wing, attributed to the heat that had sunken the week all over the country and finally brought the Ranch to its knees; which sprung Cleo off the walls, slapping bean bags in their wake. Cash, we needed cash. I was supposed to look for it earlier in the week but forgot as soon as he'd asked, and now we needed it bad.

"We can just rip up some paper," said Germaine. Cleo scoffed.

"How can someone so beautiful say something so evil," they said. I agreed. Sacrilege. So we took Germaine's car because it had self-drive and we were blasted. Cleo entered stops for three gas stations, starting a game where we would pull in and they'd slow the speed to a crawl, then we took turns diving out, searching for an ATM, or begging an attendant, then sprinting back before the car hit the road and jumped to 90 miles an hour. The first three had nothing so we lit a joint and punched in five more in a pentagram.

"Call the Blaze Team!" Cleo hung their head out the window and whooped at the black plains feeding the blue night.

We got seventy-two singles in exchange for a hundred at the fourth in the pentagram, which hid itself in a box of ferns and the old, sterile, white lights of purgatory. Any invented white is a disturbing imitation of the moon's grace.

I was on my back, sprawled three seats out remembering the first time I saw the ocean. Cleo's third ankle slap got me out and he said it was impolite to enter sim with company. We were back at the Ranch, behind a coach bus bespeckled in vibrant pastels. The beat hit then, shivering the metal around us, and Cleo couldn't wait anymore and threw me fifteen singles on his way in. I caught up in the east hall but Cleo threw themselves into the foyer.

Masc, Your Aide kicked above his head to drop, roll over, scissor, before making the rounds for tips. Cleo burst in a shower of singles. We screamed and pounded the walls, starving for more. The music cut to sampled dialogue and we roared. He tousled his mullet then noticed his bicep, slapped it again and again, pointed to the door frame before leaping into a set, two sets, three sets of pull-ups and Cleo was in love; it burned on their face and wracked the body. The king slipped out while Helen the Toy took stage. She was bubble gum bimbo that set everyone on edge, pawing at what they could, and I lost half my singles to her.

Kris taught me and Cleo how to play baseball. Neither of us liked how fast she threw it, but she said that was the only way we'd learn, so we had to stand there and have her whip it at us and try to launch it away. A few others played, but there still wasn't enough for two teams.

"It drops in the outfield and Cleo has to sling it to Moss, who gets it to third, but Germaine's already rounding to home so she's stuck between them and Simon, back and forth and she's gotta make a move. God! It could be so great." She shook Wells. "Why don't you all play."

"Different strokes, baby."

"I know, I know. Just dreaming."

Germaine had her head on a pillow, arms draped across the scorched rugs. The space was an extension of her. "You know when you're with someone, all close and in their face, and it has nothing to do with them anymore because you're breathing the same breath so they could be your lover or your enemy so long as you stay in it, and you realize everyone breaths the same, that it's all the same, so there's no real difference and it could be your lover or your enemy and you can't tell. It's like that. 'Cause the greatest thing you've ever known is just the same as the worst so you can't help but think of one with the other."

"I don't see the issue," said Cleo. Germaine was exhausted though, settling with what she'd said.

Wells picked it up. "But that passes and you're left with whatever you brought in. Have you ever ended laughing? Like a running joke." The lights bloomed from deep red to purple. I wanted to think I knew what he meant. "I know where you are. It's exhausting. It passes though, and the real thing comes. And it'll go. Just stay what you're in, I guess."

~

The Blaze Team knew grilling, naturally. It was on the driveway of Kevin's place that they insisted Orion and I get them funding. The idea being they could work sections of Redfield until the whole thing was gone and they'd be heroes. I tried to describe the Memphis team losing ground but they wouldn't hear it. Jerry explained that they didn't know the land they were burning, that that team was from all over, that *they* knew Redfield and knew how to deal with it all properly. I said all they knew was how to hold their beer, and we laughed, and I hoped that would be the end of it until we left.

A dozen kids ran around the yards, coming out front to dive into the kiddie pool or wolf a hot dog before so-and-so needed them for a secret mission out back and the parents raised their eyebrows and urged them to get on it. A couple boys played Blaze Team with the hose, dousing the lawn then each other and "melting."

Orion parked it in a lawn chair under the big cedar because they promised Kevin's daughter they would braid her hair, and it kept them away from the Blaze Team who they still called nuts to their faces, but the Team laughed and said it would be different when Orion came back next year. Kevin's place was a classic sort with a wide, screened porch in front, and a roof that peaked like an arrow. It was yellow all around by then and warm so it was going to be a hot autumn. The cicadas roared louder than I'd ever heard and I thought they'd lift us all into the giant stretch of pink and blue above.

A couple more girls wandered over to Orion's spot which concerned some moms until they went over and were just as charmed, and I chuckled. This circle of lawn chairs on the driveway had wrangled me in to talk about the country and people these days. It was *all going to hell, you see.* And *soon the crazies would come.* Which reminded me of Trevor's *duhn duhn duhn* holes in the wall. But I wasn't going to tell ghost stories.

"They're already here," said Jerry. "I don't let my Kayla *or* Brad drive down Kennel. Now as a father, you expect to have to worry about your daughter no matter where you are, but hell, some of those fairies are huge."

"What's the deal?" I asked.

"You know," he said. "There's this big black one, no offense Charles, comes into the store sometimes — hungry look on 'em."

"Ah."

"Now I voted for Obama, Ann can attest, so you wanna shoot up in a ditch and take it where it doesn't shine, fine, but that's what cities are for."

"Huh."

"Well you tell me, would you feel safe having your kids grow up around that?"

"Not sure I'll have kids."

"You know what I mean."

"Sure."

"So would you?"

"I do." He laughed.

"Well, hey, that just proves my point. You can be whatever you are without being *that*."

"Gotcha." I got up and swished the ice around, pointed to the beer by the house.

Simon loved working his own projects because they were new and unbroken. The Ranch always had some part to mend, and it would never end. This door jam, that siding, her doorknob, etc. But the days he didn't fix anything was when he chewed cuticles and paced. An energy that had to be displaced, given over to some disorder. A stick he'd always retrieve. So I saw why Kris poked him; how he lured her. The slightest shift in the foundation, a quiet day, and a new machine was in motion, pinballing them off each other until it resettled. I thought of how someone described a dead body, *disturbingly still*. No breath. Simon would never stop breathing, even when he died. He gave it somewhere else so some part was always in motion, his ripple.

"The best furniture's never sold," said Simon.

"How so?" I found myself talking different around him. Combinations resurfacing.

"It's being sold, so you can't take much satisfaction in making it."

115

"There's a paycheck."

"Yeah, and the promise of more. Not a great reason to do your best."

"So what happens to the best?"

"It's given."

"Corny."

"It's true."

"Corny."

"If you sell it, most you get is pride in a job well done, and that will take you a while, but trust me, it's hollow." Simon sanded the birdhouse in quick strokes. "Because it's either already sold, or you need to make it look like it should be. When you make it for love, every move is made to an ideal. It's unreal. Might crush it with how perfectly you want to shape it, scanning every seam. Flourishes you've never considered come to mind because it's *for* someone. And they tell you how to make it, in their way. So you show them this monument you made out of their light, how you thought they might like a chair, a table, a nightstand. We're way past 'best' I suppose. Best is the lowest common denominator, and this is so specific, it's far beyond." I thought about Marijean plating dinner, how unnecessary it was, how she insisted. Had I ever eaten better? He looped a string through the top of the house, set it on the hook hanging in the back corner of his station by the window. Cleo and I promised to paint it later, suddenly a more deliberate task. "I hate that tree," said Simon. He pointed out the window. It pressed its ferns against the glass, blocking out all light.

"Listen, when I bought this house, I had a dream of what the lawn might look like. See, my Dziadzu kept this pristine Mother Mary in the corner of his lawn — stepping stones, a candle holder and everything. This little station where anyone in the neighborhood could stop by. On Christmas Eve, people came from three towns over to pray by it together. So when I bought this place, I knew I needed that. I'm not religious myself, but a place to go, you know? And the lawn's big enough so why not. See that over there?" He pointed to a clump of bushes surrounding a slanting pile of wood. "The gazebo's inaccessible how it is now." Prairie grass went up through the tawny blanks. I could tell he had tried cutting it down by how it hewed in a straight line. "And people come for Independence Day and it's a big deal. I think if I had some funding I could keep it clear permanently."

This was an easier case. I forwarded him one of the pamphlets: Indigenous Grass and Your Lawn — A Win for Everyone. He looked at it a while, just the front page.

"Ok," he said.

"I'm sorry, it's just the outside area, you know?"

"Right. Thanks for coming by." He didn't offer his hand when I left.

~

There was singing somewhere in the east wing. It rang more than it should have. I tracked it down to an extension from the porch, a bright, hot room with windows open on all sides. Six of them in total. The tenor I recognized as Moss. Frankie stood in front of the five with a dinky keyboard that was turned up all the way but the sound still flew out the windows.

"Each has to think they are the only one in the song — the melody. If they think about the others they lose their potency, they become enmeshed, wanting to mingle with one another, and it's this dissonant nightmare. So I separate them. Record each part individually, then push them together in post so they can hear what it's supposed to sound like. So we have this sonically perfect chord, but now it sounds like shit. Can't tell you why it sounds like shit because they're more in tune, more their part, but it sounds like shit. They're missing each other's tone and shape. We call that *blend*. So it's another week of that, then maybe we can add some style before show night. And even then you're lucky if they put on a good performance, because Len's already tired of the song and just pushing through, and Hugo's been worried about their partner all day, so then it's my job to get them all right *here* and forgetting everything they know while remembering everything we went over without actually thinking about any of it and hope it just carries them until the end. And even then it might sound like shit because who knows, but however it ends they're all happy, and the audience hates it, so who knows why we do it." Harmony. Had never really known what that meant. Seemed silly to go so long without knowing what that extra thrum was. Moss hated being a tenor because it meant either a weak melody or a floating top line. Basses had all the fun, pounding away.

The nice part about the west wing was it let out into the garden from the patio. The Ranch was a puzzle box fitted together on whims over the years, so there wasn't much *flow*. But it let people fill space fully. Too long in any one room and the whole place might tip, staring too close, granular. Move on though and the place breathed — give you didn't know you were waiting for. I wanted to pick up the whole place and spin it around like a Rubik's cube.

There were two picnic tables in the back of the Ranch that they used to put together to make a stage but a rosebush grew through the center of each now. Everyone blamed Moss, but they were adamant it wasn't them who planted it, though they smiled when they denied it, which still didn't say much because Moss was always showing teeth when you were looking. So we had to sit backward on the benches and fit plates on our laps or between thorns. The year before Cleo planted a couple saplings nearby so there were two birches to keep us cool. Jenna warned them that if they kept planting she might just call the

Blaze Team to make room.

"Must be a lot easier out here." I gestured at the rows of garden beds. What looked like tomatoes spun around the nearest trellis. Lines of peas started below and hooked onto the Ranch's roof, creating a canopy when you walked out.

"Oh, you've never had a garden," said Kris. "Growing's never the hard part — it's everything else that grows. Even the stuff you want. Wells' strawberries would choke the whole plot if I let them."

"Just think of the cakes," said Wells.

"I know babe, I know."

I noticed the underbrush now, how it hiked up so there was a clear line end to end. Noticed the spacing where I'd perceived a monolith.

"What if you didn't prune?" I asked.

"It'd eat itself," said Kris.

"Could you grow it all wild?"

"Sure, but we'd use a lot more space then."

"Be more natural."

"Sure, and Wells can go gut a bison."

Cleo laughed when I told them about the Blaze Team. They were upstanding citizens who torched their yards. How dare they be beset by queers. Cleo went on like this a while, *the hicks*, and I remembered he was smart enough to not say any of

120

it in front of them, but I knew that didn't matter. They were exactly what they thought of each other, which gave them both an outlet. We roared around the east wing that night. A group just got back from a backpacking trip in Yellowstone and wanted us to experience it through their sims. I was belaying down a cliff face above a torrent of white, trying to make the outcropping — just a couple feet. The rope flitted through faster than anticipated and my legs were swept left in the current, breaking my head over the surface. I felt bubbles of clean snowpack in my throat. Then I was flailing in the Horowitz's basement, hoping Rachel would push down on my throat to stop it all, then I was swinging on Germaine's black hole of a carpet before finding the off switch.

"What was that dude," said Cleo. "I was about to pull you out." I apologized and found some weed.

We were out on the pond raft, lit up so ghosts curled around the gibbous. There used to be some meaning to the phases, but that didn't sound right. It sounded like something Sci made up for a lesson. When I put my head down I could hear the reeds growing into skyscrapers. Cleo was talking to someone, the one they swore at, but in a gentle tone, like they might reconcile. This turned bitter though and they beat the planks of the raft and I shouldn't have said anything but I did and then it was me, shoved for this or that and the car back in Austin. Then it really was me, for being a no-good son of a bitch, using people and preying on them since the day we met and talking shit about them to the Blaze Team and bitching all the time about Sci, and no, I didn't talk shit but *don't you say a fucking word* and I took it for a bit before swimming back to shore. I might've walked back to the motel if I wasn't such a coward but instead laid down on Cleo's floor. They woke me a few hours later to apologize. They were just hurt I would even associate with them, and I understood, and after they dropped me off the next morning we never spoke again.

Orion loved the Ranch but couldn't go back after fighting with Bertie, a TERF.

"That's fucked," I said.

"I know," said Orion. "She's not even part of a coven."

I was working a job in town, among the bushes of streetlights near the edge of the Hawthorn yard. Orion found a weedkiller a few towns away that worked better than anything we'd used so far, so we stocked up on it, and I sprayed conservatively up to the house. The door was always swinging closed with some family member coming or going. There was a great debate over whether to sell the farm since Mom's passing. Usual back and forth about tradition and autonomy. They tried to get me to weigh in a couple times, so I finally played the Yankee talking about hydroponics and how it could make a nice nature preserve and they let me alone.

"You know the difference between someone that's learned to cook by hand and someone that's taken lessons?" Marijean was chopping red onions for guacamole.

"Hm?"

"Professionals teach you to cut fast. Consistently. An even cook and all. But it gets a little lost if you ask me." The knife slid wet through the rings. She set them on their side and made an X. "You want maybe 90% the same. Maybe 80. The rest gotta be a bit bigger, a bit smaller."

"How come?"

"Chunks reminds you it's there, what it's doing for the dish. The smaller ones just blend nicer." She snacked on them, so did I.

"Everyone wants what we have," Cleo had said.

"What? The Ranch?"

"People. That's what they can't stand, more than anything. All the faces coming and going, opposing, and we're still here. They'd all join if they could. But it's not so easy. And they hate that, so they want to see us broken up. Tale as old as time."

"They've got their own people."

"Ha! Sure. Built on what though? A place? That's not enough. Go long enough and they'll all be tearing each other's throats. It's not just them though. See it everywhere you go. Somebody at the outside of the circle trying to edge their way in. Like they can't just leave a group alone, you know? They think just because you've taken in so many others, what's one more? It's annoying. Leeches. Rather than making something themselves."

All these perfect memories I couldn't touch. I needed to distract myself, put on a sim, the most mindless loot-feed-sim I could find and lost a week in it, until I emerged and had forgotten about it all entirely, could walk around the neighborhood and marvel at the patterns on leaves. Yes, that was real and more important than anything and everything else was a distraction. If I found a distraction for every bad moment then I could look back and laugh at my self-importance. Such silly connections. Things that would never mean a thing again. One-offs. Blow through town over and over again. Blind me to the possibility.

I slept. I was behind the wheel, driving without thinking. Following some path. I could only see the turn when it was right in front of me, then I was careening around, sliding near the ditch, back in place, forward. Maddening. I couldn't slip out of the turn, nor make it earlier. Side streets were window-dressing. And I knew it was coming, that every time I thought it would happen it wouldn't. So I forgot about it and it did. The car tilted on the last turn, going over the edge and it shot through me, the jolt, and I woke up.

I think the problem with me and Sci was we were always out in the open where historically good things get killed. There was no room to long while it sat simply, so it smothered in the air.

They filled my head with all this nonsense then vanished. Each piece floating through with their imprint. Whatever came next might be lesser.

We stopped by a couple more towns in South Dakota, each deader than Redfield, for which by then I was grateful. Overbrook came into focus again, without a pull. I figured this was what I needed from Overbrook — a place to keep fixed no matter how desperately I wanted to escape so when I was really out I could become grateful and comfortably spiteful.

Orion came into the car on our way to Montana with ice white hair. I told them it looked good; they nodded. They were consigned to dying alone, as we all do, and for this I respected them more than anyone I'd known. I fooled myself now and then — accepting this inevitability rather than facing it, and here Orion was, gliding in a note until it dropped off the face of the earth. Any desolation had hardened into clarity, through which they saw us for what we were.

There were stretches I forgot either of us were in the car, becoming so involved in the landscape that my consciousness was just a reel of green and blue in increasingly familiar silhouettes; a lane change might bring me back but Orion did so with an ease I knew as a consequence of the same delirium. They hummed a half dozen grey notes.

# Part Three

In Clearview, Montana the rain started at 3:32 PM and stopped at 5:54 PM, every day. Anything from a mist to fat columns that fell straight down. Always the same time. Pools filled among the mousy sagebrush. Farmers tried introducing more corn, cotton, and rice, but the plains flooded before anything could take root. Sci wanted to go — something about a greater chance of mutation out of adaptation. They had to hit Nebraska though, which had less water and deeper root systems. Orion kept calling Montana West. I said Midwest. That kept us entertained for a few hours.

"So what's Kentucky?" I asked.

"South all the way," they said.

"No, same latitude as Virginia."

"Yeah, why do you think West Virginia exists?"

"Same as Dakota or Carolina — infighting."

"They kept slavery!"

"This is culture, not history."

"Which doesn't come out of nothing, you dip. Antebellum South was a real thing."

"Really? Thought they made it up for the movies."

"Oh fuck off."

Summer loitered, dogging September. I thought of Grayson and what it looked like when everything died. I wished I asked Sci more Overgrowth questions. Only after leaving did I know what I wanted to know. I wasn't even sure it got cold down in Wynne.

"How did you know I am what I am?" I asked.

Their questioning grunt.

"On the way to Spencer," I said. I looked out the passenger window. "You said I had to stay in shape, show up when I said — not give them a reason."

"Oh." They clicked their tongue. "Knew it from the first night, the motel. You wouldn't make eye contact. You wouldn't push me, even when I tried to make you."

"Plenty of people like that."

"You're a different type, sure, but I've been around — I know it when I see it."

"Uh-huh."

"You'll get there."

The first storm in Clearview I walked under a raincoat I had stolen from Germaine. I meant to grab my flannel, so it was a happy accident. I messaged Germaine about it just in case, but she never got back to me. The clouds broke into onyx shrapnel that streaked across the sky. Curtains of rain *plap*ed off the leaves. Grass sea ripe. Every breath clean. The deserted streets seemed normal. Like people were staying in from the rain. Fewer houses, but better kept. There were a few soft, yellow lights on, framed in foliage I thought I could live in. I wondered what else there might be. Something that could enjoy food I think, that was about all I knew. And maybe seasons, to watch it all move around. Over and over, and then I knew it was a mad summer. I wasn't ready to sleep but by the end I might be. The retreat, back to rest. Start again later. I imagined heaps of frozen leaves caked to the ground, to be eaten in the spring, ripened, mulch. It was winter and the ponds had frozen over so it was a tundra of ice pockets. Snow now, so I stuck my tongue out and caught some drops and more slid down my jacket, down my back. Now I knew where we were going, end to end, good and bad. Couldn't see how it would end though. I always want to end on a high note. But who knows. It seemed so obvious. It was just a choice, an option. I had to jump, pick one, or it would storm forever and pick me up and drop me all over until I dropped. Would the

Ranch take me? Overbrook. But it was thousands of miles away and moving without me, and I needed to see someone in the rain: driving a car, across the street, anything. The rain would never stop, just flood the whole place, and I wanted to ask Sci what might happen. They wanted to be there.

I left my shoes on the porch. The sun came through the wide window onto Orion and the L couch. Nelson bounded around the corner, down the hall to me. She patted my thighs back and forth real quick.

"Good girl, good to see you."

Orion picked her up on the road. Some guy with a truck for $50 a piece. Orion didn't know if they'd keep her but figured it was better than her being on the road, and we were moving, so why not, she'd go somewhere. She had some lab in her, chocolate, with a beagle snout. Nelson from Willie Nelson, who Orion wasn't too familiar with but it sounded like a name that belonged out there. Orion took her out on jobs and let her loose to run in the fields or yards. I wondered how many pets they'd had so far.

"Does it taste funny?" asked Orion. I laid my coat carefully on the hook.

"Couldn't tell. Rain always tastes funny, yeah?"

"Yeah, I guess."

The rain cooled the whole house and it was summer and brighter for a while.

There was a grill out back so we made burgers and corn. They were full ground beef and the buns were toasted. Orion threw Nelson an orange frisbee across the weeded backyard. There were fewer jobs out there, farther between and cut off sometimes from flooding, so we made lunch when we could. Sometimes Orion called a buddy and we didn't talk much. Then they'd tell me about their sister in Arizona, their work in private equity, the summer in Mongolia. I tried to listen for a thread, some throughline, but couldn't find one, as if their life fell before them.

Charlene was a project manager, building custom McMansions across the Midwest. Her client wanted a gaudy "ranch" away from Detroit.

"And they draw these little cartoons of everything they want, like 'oh you just pass these to the AI hur-dur-dur!' So I waste all my time explaining no, AI's for prefab you dink, but what do I fucking care — I'll build a buttress out of their wife's thong if they pay for it."

Her team lived out of a dozen vans parked along the perimeter of the site. They had made a pitch with leftover paint and were playing when I first arrived. The rain hit when I finished my initial assessment. The two dozen men ran after each other to the vans. One locked his buddy out who laughed and banged on theirs then their neighbor's doors before running over to the tent where Charlene was.

"Hey Jelly, looks like it's just you and me," he said.

"Perfect," said Charlene. "I've got some messages you can help answer."

"Oh fuck no."

The foundation got swamped, or cracked under new growth every few days. Charlene wanted my expertise and offered cash to stick around and spray, so I did, between further jobs that weren't worth the drive. They'd all stop what they were doing if they spotted a weed and make way for me like a prophet to cut it down. I learned something about comedic timing — relearned what'd starting coming back in Redfield. A joke had to be sat on, because it was always going to be better. The first opening was never the best, and the more we talked the better I got at waiting for the next. And sometimes the moment would pass entirely, the joke with it, and that was more cathartic because the talk was going somewhere better, and it must've not been that good a joke anyways if it didn't rise between our pauses, slip into the offbeat. The rhythm of our conversation.

The best nights were movie nights because everyone got off early, and it was Friday. And the movie sucked, but Charlene looked the other way if they played with the equipment, so they made concrete shoes and had races, *cinder foot*, or shot up the cedar with the nail gun, *barkgammon*. I stayed a couple times but the movie really did suck, and the games seemed more dangerous than the Blaze Team.

I was walking to a claim where the shrubs pushed out from the crawlspace, through the underside of the porch, so the whole place rested on a green foundation. It was one of the few that might see some money. The sidewalks were gone so I walked down the center of the road, waved wide at oncoming cars. Ahead there was a bend that turned to the sun, like a door down the hall in the middle of the night. The shade was forgiving, but I wanted to sprint to the turn. A fear if I did the sun would set right then and there. So I walked. I got there and watched the split, the shadow and the gold. Down the center was a stone — granular, smooth, enough weight in my palm — and I pocketed it.

Summers were supposed to be cooler when Mom was a kid, and I didn't believe her until I started reminiscing about cooler summers. There were dog days Danny and I were holed up, sure, but these days it just didn't let up. Fall was always a little nicer, that's a plus. So's Winter — that's worrying. It had the effect where the lighter it was outside, the longer I'd have to stay in during the day. The more sitcoms we'd watch. Orion remembered more than I did, but they were familiar faces and that was enough to keep me on that couch, blinds drawn. We'd wake up and let Willie Nelson out, have breakfast in the yard under the shadow of the house. Our little island. The yard went a half mile long, maybe thirty feet wide, though Orion called Nelson back if they went too deep in the tall grass near the end of the fence. Some fear about coyotes or snakes. Then it'd get to where we couldn't ignore the heat, saw the shimmer between the plain and sky, and we threw the utensils and plates into the brush. I closed the blinds while Orion set the air conditioner and arranged the blankets.

Any P-51 Mustangs worth anything were in a museum. Frank got them in Oshkosh for a song. They were memorabilia for a while, then show planes, then trophies, then collector's items, then worthless. He got me in the cockpit with the cracked leather, and it reminded me of Orion's car. It angled up, pulling me back, setting my sights.

"Feels real enough to be fake," I said.

"Oh, it's the real deal. See in the Pacific they needed this gauge here and you don't see that in replicas."

I chuckled. "No, I know, I know."

"How does this always happen to you?" asked Orion.

I shrugged. "People like talking about what they like. If you let them go long enough, they'll probably show you."

"Yeah, I think that's the problem."

"I don't know. I think we end up spending more time alone than we think. Makes you want to hear someone else when you get a chance."

Frank lost his kid in the war. He was proud of it, *only good way to die*. Sometimes he talked to him, so I guess he hadn't really left. They talked about the economy and open borders. It was reach in a different way, so I didn't judge it much. Everyone wanted some ideal beyond them and got all torn up that it didn't exist. Suppose I was reaching in another way. The secret ways I was afraid to name, that they'd pinball far, far away. Maybe that's what Frank and his son were doing too — floating around it.

"No one has religion anymore," said Frank. "That's the problem."

"I think it scared people."

"Damn straight."

"But they didn't care about being good, they were just scared."

"That's not true. Wouldn't have gone as long as it did if that was true."

"Yeah, because people made money off it."

"Well sure, what can't you? I'm just saying: it was a bunch of people getting together to say they wanted to be nice."

"Never made sense to me. Just forever and ever as ourselves. Don't think we would be the same, so what's the difference. 'We' are never in heaven."

"We are for a bit, then we're something greater. Place where things just get better."

"But it'll snap back. The longer it goes on, the sooner it's hell. All good necessitates all evil, so a heaven's existence inherently damns."

"Extremes are choices. You let the world act on you, yeah, you're in that middle, bit of it all, flown to the winds, back and forth. You want to be bad? The worst? Doesn't happen on its own. Respect the choice, because it lets others be so good."


I called Mom. She wanted to know everything about what it was like out there, and I told her about the vines and grass. I expected her to press more but she didn't, so I let more slip about Orion and Yates, and she chuckled when she should have.

"Sounds like quite the adventure," she said.

"Might be a life."

"Oh, well I could see why. All that life." And who knows if I'd ever go back. I thought I would until that conversation.

I ran a sim for a while: I was the captain of a spaceship, negotiating a boarding party. A tentacle creature pleaded I consider all perspectives and the answer was obvious. I was utilitarian. Least harm principle. I let them board us, and when they slaughtered half the crew I at least had the consolation that

I had saved more lives. It was over before I had made the choice, and I set the OnBoard on the nightstand. Whatever happened next was far more intriguing. So I sat and waited, but no one came to the door and I passed the whole night alone like that. Tomorrow was another day so it didn't matter.

My arms ached. Six months of hacking and boiling hadn't developed the pillars I thought they might. These were two wire bundles fraying at the end. I pleaded to whatever was above for an empty home, for a dead body that would curse me and my entire family. Anything but the burning rips in my triceps, the knot bunching in my back. And the people were as dim as Wynne, welcoming and excited that their pleas had been answered out there in the middle of nowhere where we both knew they were alone. I imagined the strength of Wells, Atlas, the fire of the Blaze Team, tearing through the living room. When I finished I wanted to weep because the next house was a short walk away. Yes, the walks were a reprieve, just as much as they mocked. These verdant roads that stretched simply in the sun, thankful for its harshness. They shaded. Offered clean breezes. No, they were not my enemies. But they did nothing to assuage my fear that they would be back, wherever I went. I couldn't join them, not yet, we both knew. *Contraction.* I wished Sci could see how taught I was, worn.

~

I bought some groceries and tried to recreate the pasta Marijean always did, but the sauce was soup and made the chicken sopping, and I could've finished it but just the sight upset me because I knew what it was supposed to be, so I dumped it and Dropped food. Sat on the couch with Orion and watched an old show they liked.

"It's never like this," said Orion. "Just a bunch of friends hanging out. For what?"

"Think I've been there."

"Sure, when you're a kid. They put you with everyone so something happens. But you grow up and it's just you and maybe a partner."

"Yeah." But why watch something you lived?

The plants in the corner were getting taller and I knew I could've taken care of them but I knew Orion hadn't done it in a while and they probably never would so why should I. We didn't live there anyways. Maybe I'd steal some light bulbs for the hell of it.

*Starts somewhere.* I kept hearing it to where I thought I was going crazy. I asked Orion what it meant and they must have thought I was high, and then I really thought I was crazy because I wasn't high and that didn't seem like a crazy question. I knew what it meant, but not why everyone kept saying it.

"Who's everyone?" Orion asked.

"Like in passing, on jobs. I think you've even said it

before."

"I definitely haven't."

"You've never said 'it starts somewhere' before?"

"No, that doesn't even make sense."

"Yes it does. Like, you want to fix a car. Starts somewhere."

"What starts?"

"Fixing it!"

"Well either it's busted or its fixed."

"It can't be fixed overnight, so you've gotta *start somewhere*."

"Yeah," they said. "I get it. But until it works again, it's busted. Whatever happens before doesn't matter. Broken or fixed." Every time I wanted to pull out Orion would say some other ridiculous thing that pulled me in, and I didn't even think they believed it half the time; and when I wasn't pulled in they'd say something else I couldn't resist, even more ridiculous, and we'd be back at it. I was exhausted. I was fighting as someone else, some primal kick against not the topic but the argument itself, willing Orion to shut it, until I finally walked away. But they followed me to my room, knocked on the door.

"Why are you being so sensitive? It's just a debate."

"I'm going to bed."

An hour later they started sending me articles, and I thought I was going crazy.

It was raining when I woke up, and I remembered rain in the night. A grey wall that hid everything but the shrubs in front of the windows. I stayed in bed awhile, going through old messages with Sci until I felt ridiculous and started deleting them. The sound of Nelson pattering around. Her low whine. I got up. She was pushing her nose against Orion's door.

"C'mon girl." I let her out. She bounded around the yard, catching as much water in her smile as she could. I held her through the towel when she came in. She turned around just to whack me in the face with her tail.

Orion tried Dropping breakfast but the drone must have been crushed in the torrent because it never came. We laid on the couch a while, watching the storm change. Guessed what brought the rain: a military machine, one of the horsemen, another Overgrowth incidental. All over the world it would rain and rain and never stop but the earth would keep soaking it up and we'd find a way to convert it into power and skincare and that would be life, so we accepted the rain and resigned to rot there. Orion went to their room and beckoned Nelson, shut the door. It was getting bright enough to sleep. Dreamt. I was on a stairwell in a basement with people I didn't recognize. They laughed but I couldn't hear the joke so I laughed too. The party went on beneath us and I couldn't decide which was the better spot to be so I stood a bit and woke up. The light hadn't changed so I turned my head and watched the rain. A few years ago I might've been in a sim even before I got up. Who's to say this was better. I clicked my OnBoard and scrolled but found nothing interesting. How it had devolved so fast I'll never know. A falling sky was preferable. And I watched the rain with a soft smile. In and out of sleep. And Alex was there too — breath a rolling wave. Yes, I could live here.

The principal caught me in a bar. She was sneaky about it too, asking where I was from and what brought me out there. By then I didn't tell people I was on Overgrowth unless specifically asked, but she had gotten a few in me, and I was waking up for school the next day. When I arrived, Principal Kacey was hacking at the shrubs in the entrance to the asymmetric two-story building. An arch had been cut out and maintained with trellises. She said every morning she redirected the vines to move further along the trellises. It was part of her routine, which included yoga, coffee, then walking her dog to the school. It smelled sweeter than I remembered but still had that base note of sweat baked into the murky blue carpet, tangled with oxygen. The principal brought me upstairs where the vines thinned, so far from the dirt. It was a loft really, an annex added on in the 20s for Montana's population boom. There were four classrooms and one teacher's lounge. Each classroom had a "Plant Wall" opposite the window, interwoven with photos of kids with tiny shovels, holding a seedling in their palm, or their arms outstretched, eyes closed, hugging the wall. Otherwise, the shrubs, vines, and grass were reigned to the corners or edges.

"How many kids do you have here?" I asked.

"Eleven across five years: first, third, fourth, sixth, and eighth" she said. "We joined up with the middle school last year."

"Damn. All in-sim, huh."

"No, Montana Charter."

Montana Charter rode the alternative learning wave in the oughts to become the premier charter school in Montana. The state struck a deal years back to provide subsidized tuition for residents, poaching families until small schools like Kacey's were the only public option left. There was a county vote every couple years to cut the public schools' budget which always passed. Kacey said a trillionaire owned Montana Charter and hated teachers.

Schools weren't on our list because they were community-owned, and therefore a local-federal discussion above my pay grade. Kacey walked me through each classroom and told me the personalities of Josie, and Ava, and Maurice, and Glen, and what they wanted to be, and I got the idea and said I'd be back with weedkiller.

It took the whole week to make it through the first floor, even with Kacey's help. I showed her how to find the roots of shrubs without digging around the soil, then how to flood the halls in a boil. It surprised me how much I could verbalize the process, and she would look far off and nod while I explained then ask a flurry of clarifying questions until she could stoop and rip up a fern with one hand. Every day she started by retreading the areas we had weeded and even had her dog, Clarence, pee in the sunnier corners.

Kacey grew up there and thought she'd run away to be a nurse in some big city until her dad made her take a daycare job to help with rent. Her oldest, Nate, was in Phoenix and wouldn't be coming back, and her husband was a wonder, content.

We started at 6:00 am because she was determined to enjoy at least the end of her summer. Prickled moss surrounded the art room, except in the shadow of a young spruce. It was an oblong of bristles that refused to die. I snipped branches off first to get an angle on the trunk then hacked with the hatchet I picked up in Redfield. Kacey whirled around with clumps of moss. The spruce raked me with each windup, loosing blood fast in the hyperfocus that ensued. Only every third chop made a dent, and I beat it, beat it, beat it, because we were so close and it was getting hot.

"You ok, hon?" She touched her hand to the small of my back and the charge sent me.

"Yeah," I said. "Tough thing." She had finished the moss and was working the ferns, the spruce becoming an outlier. "We can torch it."

Her face flashed concern before affecting consideration

and I wanted to cry right there for how she looked at me all bloodied with a hatchet and I remembered what Orion said. Kacey had some loon with her she had to appease and I almost did want to chop her up out of self-pity for what she said.

"That's a good idea. But the smoke alarms might go off then it'll be a whole thing. So how about we finish the day and brainstorm for tomorrow?"

I imagined the thing burning in the center of the room, worried it was arcane and would burn eternally as the giant wick of the art room.

Kacey took me out to dinner afterward and asked me questions that got me talking and she looked at me the way my mom or favorite teachers used to, a knowing placidness, and I wanted to cry all over again, and I thanked her for dinner too many times.

I was exhausted by then and loathsome because there it was again and there it went, so I hiked it to the edge of town to my favorite dive and got a double. It was a still night made all the sorrier by me being there because people can sense that kind of thing when they're as spiritually attuned as the people in a dive. Water and beer pooled by the door like it did in every other dead ditch in town.

Willie Nelson got out when we were helping clear a tree

in the middle of the road. When she came back, there was blood all over her jowls, around the slobbering smile. She looked stronger too, legs defined, and from then on always crouched, ready to run.

Most roofs were green but didn't need any attention. The moss or grass or weeds soaked up what came down, and though everything else was a nightmare, people liked the thatching. Made them feel like hobbits.

But Maria Webster's roof had a cedar seedling. A little antenna. It wasn't until it rained that she noticed the roots in the upstairs hall, the sag around it. By the end of the season it would be taller than her and slam through to soil.

We worked a pulley system around the top rung of the ladder so I didn't have to go down to fill up the pot every time. Maria kept a fire going on the lawn so she could walk up to the cauldron, ladle the water into the giant orange bucket, drag it across to the ladder, clip it, and pull it inch by inch up to me. I'd tried scraping everything off with a hoe first but she could hear the shingles slip, and I tried to deny it, until we watched a couple slide off, so we had the bucket. Maria was nice though. She had this bit where she'd moan about how heavy the bucket was, how afraid she was of dropping it all over herself, almost screaming as it inched to the top. But it was empty. It got me the first time, the second time I was annoyed, so she figured she'd really get me the fourth time, and by the sixth something clicked, and I laughed so hard I thought I'd roll right off the roof.

"You're much more fun than the others," said Maria.

"Others?"

"Yeah they came by the other day. Couldn't have been more than 10 minutes."

Orion and I took the whole case load for an area and split it when we rolled in. I double-checked the file and sure enough another team had closed it. I hadn't given much thought to the other teams. Orion alluded to them like dead relatives. A rush overcame me that I later realized was excitement.

Howard put me in touch with them: Tanner and Becca. We met at a diner by the highway. Orion was busy.

"So what's the coolest place you've seen?" I asked. We were waiting for our food.

"What do you mean?" said Tanner. He was the senior.

"Like plants that grew in weird ways. Or places that took on whatever was around." I told them about the maple in the supplement building.

"Oh, sure. We've seen stuff like that."

"There was this lake where algae started forming shapes," said Becca. "One looked like a duck!"

"Do you think it ate one?" I asked. She laughed.

"No, algae doesn't work like that. Sorry, what's your background again?"

"What do you mean?"

"Like did you intern with the EPA or something?"

"Oh, no. I used to bartend. This is kind of between gigs I guess."

"Fun!" She smiled but a flash went over her eyes.

"How about you?"

"Well," said Becca. Tanner chuckled. Becca did too, angled to him. "Sorry, he's just heard it so many times. I studied PoliSci but interned for this Big Ag lab my senior year and fell so in love with the work. That's actually how Tanner and I met."

"Yeah, I came in as a consultant," said Tanner. "And here's this young thing with a million questions." He knew he had a nice smile. She laughed.

"So he told me about the program and has already introduced me to some EPA buds!"

"Oh they love her — nothing enviro libs want more than a starry-eyed grad."

"Well someone's gotta fix what your gen screwed up."

"No doubt you will." We ate.

A Key West buddy interned for a senator. Always said it was just talking; getting so and so to cosign on such and such bill so they could move some funds around. She and my actor friend really hit it off. Like they made the same kind of diorama in grade school. And they were easy, always smiling and nodding and down for anything. Not a second thought — forward. They did

147

good too.

I told Tanner and Becca how grateful people were for our help. How helpful they wanted to be in turn, and I realized I sounded like Howard but didn't care. Like Maria Webster and the empty bucket bit, or clearing out a dining room so a family could eat there again. Becca had that same blank look on her face, smiling, while Tanner wore his skepticism.

"How many claims have you helped out like that?" He asked.

"All of them," I said. Was I in trouble? "Not the abandoned ones, obviously." Becca watched Tanner.

"Who's your senior?"

"Orion."

"Ah, gotcha."

"What? Are we not supposed to clear it out? I always take photos and videos beforehand." The check came. Tanner grabbed it. I insisted I'd pay him, but he wouldn't hear it.

"Listen, we've helped some old ladies in our time," said Tanner. "But even then, we usually just encourage them to move out."

"Aren't we supposed to 'assist as necessary?'"

"Well, yes, but that's more a holdover from when this program first started."

"So why are we even here? Do you guys get much funding approved, 'cause I don't."

"No, you're right," Becca chimed in. "I'm writing a report on how restrictive it is. It's like they only have us out here to save face." I knew the look now — sympathy.

"So what? You guys just show up, take some photos, and leave?"

"Well, yeah," said Tanner. "Look you've hit, what? Five towns? We have to cover way more than that before the season's over."

"Why though? It's just checking a box at that point."

"Sure, but the few that actually do get funds are much better off than never getting around to them."

"I don't think they even care about the money," I said.

Tanner kind of scoffed and looked out the window. Like I was sitting across from Orion. Well fuck me. I put on a sigh of relief, thanked them again for meeting, and he was happy to move to farewells. Becca told me to connect on WLife, and I promised I would.

Orion opened things up with Jordan a few years back, before Overgrowth. Neither of them were happy, and seeing it in the other only made it worse. So they brought it up in their way and hadn't discussed it since. When Orion got back the first year, down to Florida, where they always came back, they had their suspicions.

*So, Jamie.*

*Yeah.*

And since, they hated being home and hated being on the road.

Orion didn't smoke but decided to join me that night. The back patio lights were out so the country stretched forever from our chairs. They kept the joint while they talked.

"I don't know. It's shitty, because I'll get to know someone and really like them, what they like and dislike, but then they start sharing more and more because hey, they can tell I like them, and when they do I start liking them less and less because it was all the things I didn't want to know, and they knew that, and they can tell I'm liking them less and less so they start judging me and I like them even less and it doesn't stop. Every fucking time I meet someone they seem great and there's no reason it should happen again, but then it does, and I guess that means everyone sucks and I can't take it. I just want to be around someone that isn't shit. So I stop wanting to meet people because whatever I feel in the beginning is going to get all fucked up, so it's better to just meet someone and move on."

"Do you like being alone?"

They laughed, their high, mocking one. "I'm the worst of them."

"I don't think people are like that."

"Yeah 'cause you overlook all the shit. You put up with shit people and sigh like a sad puppy. Oh poor you!"

150

"Fuck you."

"Ha! Finally!"

"This what you prefer?"

"It's honest! You've wanted to say that since day one."

"No, only after all this."

"Bullshit."

And yes, we had been working to this, in our way. Orion chose it, and somewhere, I did too. We let it sit between us. I reached out my hand and they took one more hit before passing.

"I get it, I get it." They talked more to themselves now. "I'm pushing people away because as I see their flaws I know they're seeing mine, blah blah blah." I stood up — left to right right to left. Chest to sky. Held. "It's stupid when I say it out loud, and I'm fucking sick of hearing it. But I *keep* saying it. I'm over it. I want to be over it. Fuck! Can you just go?"

"Sure."

"Thanks."

I ordered less at the bar each time until I was only asking for waters, hoping this would provide a clarity I hadn't considered. The other bar flies paid no mind, and we shared that hostile solitude.

"Well no shit!" Everyone looked at the silhouette in the doorway. Craig pointed like a rockstar and hustled over. He clapped me on the shoulders just as Trevor had done in Spencer.

The gang got split up hopping a trailer truck in Nebraska, so Craig thought he'd head north, maybe cross into Canada. He hollered recalling the bum he'd scammed in South Dakota, splayed his hands relating the woman he had to smack to get her to leave him.

"But you, you look good!" He stood and shadowboxed my arm. "You should've been out there with me, yeah, only thing I was missing. You've got that aura, you know, kinda balance to me." One-two, one-two. He bought me a couple drinks. Didn't contemplate where he got the money.

It was late, and Craig was going into detail about his old crew in Kansas City. A desperation that reached through the years kept me, though there was a limit, and I called the last round. But Craig jumped and insisted we see the digs of Montana because he was leaving the next day. So I took him to another spot on the opposite end of town where the bowling league drank.

"Fuck! I need to get *into it* tonight, you know, a real sweet little country girl haHA."

"Alright man."

"Oh we'll find someone for you too." Craig's cheeks went up past his temples in a red glow. He led with his hips, the cowboy. It worked for him.

"Fuck, look at him." He pointed to a brunet edged a little out of the bowling league. "You know he acts all high and mighty but just wants to get plowed."

"I dunno."

"Pft! I've known enough of them."

"Okay."

We hung by the bar awhile. I told him I didn't know what was left for us. Craig nodded through the glow of his OnBoard; he seemed to know what I was going to say, *oo* and *aah*ing just before I'd get to my point.

His eyes returned to me, and I said we would call it a night, but he wasn't having it. He needed *a solid lay* before hitting the road.

"Where're you sleeping?" I asked.

"With him." He pointed at the brunet.

"You can stay with me."

"Ah, sweet dear." He took my head in his hands, then clapped my right cheek. "You'll get there. Now come on."

"You can manage."

"No, no, no. I need a copilot. His friends aren't going to let him go unless they've got someone to keep them company."

"I'm good. They're all yours."

"No, you really going to let me go alone?" He gripped my shoulder, tight.

"All yours."

"What've you got better to do, huh? Sit at home and sim some garbage?" It was harder to breath with him looking at me, like it was another point of scrutiny. I wanted to stand and stretch. Instead, I bobbed my head and shrugged.

"Ah! HaHA, you're funny," said Craig. "Look around you. You really think there's anything outside that door? This is it. Sure, keep going tomorrow, and some part of you will connect this to that, but this is it. Just a scene among scenes, strung together by some imaginary arrow forward so you don't go crazy thinking how out of sorts it all is." And he was the only one I knew in the whole country.

I congratulated the team on a game well played, offered a round. How the talk died.

Craig made his intro, but I didn't hear a word from the brunet. He leaned in to the point the guy wouldn't lean away. The group carried on their conversation like I wasn't there so I dug the bar in the context of a group.

The brunet edged back into the group, which didn't deter Craig from inquiring where he lived or how he was feeling that night. This went for a while until he wouldn't acknowledge Craig, so Craig grabbed his arm and told him it was rude to ignore someone that was talking to you. A thick forearm shot across to hold Craig by his collar.

Fuck Craig.

I was pulled back and picked up by my neck and I was drowning all over and slapping the thighs of the man behind me, gurgling. Craig was yelling over all of them about bar etiquette while someone behind us yelled at the men, and the women yelled at the men, and then we were dragged outside. My man had me in a vice. I bucked, screamed, but when I stepped on his toes he pressed hard on my windpipe and I silently screamed he was killing me. The whites of my eyes leaked into the pupil, blinding. No stars. How could they kill someone with no witnesses? Poor Danny. He'd think I did this all on purpose. Maybe him and Yates would get to meet though. My head pulsed, a live wire, *contraction*; the fade, *expansion*. Once more, twice. Oh, to rest, to rest. Finally, to rest.

My tailbone, then head, hit the asphalt. Heard only my breathing for a bit, then *duhn duhn* and groans. Craig was getting kicked. Someone was leaning over me.

"Hey." His face was set. I groaned. "Hey, you're fine. Get outta here." He jerked his thumb. I held the back of my head as I sat up. It was blurry, but Craig was getting the shit kicked out of him. "We're not going to kill him."

I drooled some thanks and got up. One of them tried talking to me about their claim as I hobbled to the rental car. I grunted, then shut the door, clicked "Home," passed out.

Nelson weighed on my legs. I pulled the sheets and her close despite the pain. She drove her tongue down my ear until I pushed her neck.

"Don't do that again." Orion was in the doorway.

"I know."

"No, you don't. Or you wouldn't have done it."

"Fuck, fine, you're right, happy?"

"The fuck is that? You know how you looked in that car? Covered in vomit and shit. The car was sitting there with its lights on, and I think we're getting robbed, but no, just you fucking around again."

"*Again?*" My head throbbed but I didn't care. "Last time this happened was 'cause your psycho cuck tried to kill me." They gave a single, high laugh.

"Sure, kid."

And there I was, finally alone, because Willie Nelson knew where the food came from.

Sci was infuriating and brilliant. They changed my way of thinking so I was always orbiting them, caught in this ellipse. And I knew if I got closer the whole thing would blow up, could feel the repulsion as much as the attraction. So I came to detest their pings. These invitations to crash. To nail it down, to define it, would be death. A stagnation that would root us longer than it should, crater us so the rest of our short time would be spent crawling out of the hole. No; if I stepped back it would always be the thing that wasn't and could be anything, an unopened box, alive and dead.

They had found time to visit Clearview and its rain. A test. One I intended to pass. Yes, it wouldn't get the best of me. I would let it wash over me and move forward. And then — Sci hanging out the window, their hips against mine. Let it fade. Forget.

Orion and I spoke even less. The walks grew mournful, shuffling this way and that across the plains until they decided to take me. So it was there I saw — the whole dismal trip from start to finish and the rest of it as fertilizer. So silly then, so quaint. My feet anticipated divots and roots, and I knew the dance of Bertie the TERF — a drunken glide. My legs were emancipated, walking me over the country while my torso twisted this way and that, dodging branches; my head bobbing to some garbled melody. This was frictionless speed. A state of hysterics brought on by a full future.

There was a while I couldn't remember Yates' name, which I didn't feel guilty about; no, he'd been better off slipping my mind. It felt unfair to put a name to the last weirdo in Wynne.

Joanna Mathers talked to her plants and let me in on their secrets. The truth of the matter was they had their own wars going on, that Overgrowth had only sped it up — their industrial revolution. A tree was a local superpower to the root systems below, dictating which fungi could thrive based on how they grew their branches: to shade or not to shade. They all hated the Kudzu, had heard stories of its tear through the south and its encroach north as the winters got warmer. It would suffocate them all, and we didn't even care. *Green blindness.* All green was good to humans. But the grasses reminded everyone of our care, what that really meant, and a fight against the Kudzu was better than our attention. We were best left lulled, to walk our paths in the assumed passivity. Our motives beyond comprehension. The wisest among them was the wintergreen. Steadfast year round and helpful to humans, but inconvenient in too large of quantities. Pretty enough to seem deadly. Native. The fungi were admired and feared. They bore news from the coasts and Africa, on the wind or under the ocean, mycelium deeper than any roots. And while this oak or that elm might thwart their expansion, they always had other routes. Whispers said they would cover the world when we succumbed. But for now they were governed by whatever bully of a tree stood in their way, that tree in turn spaced perfectly from the next so they might not war over light — yet. The stasis we perceived was a privilege.

I got back from a walk, but it was a bad day, and I remembered why I had gone on it in the first place. Orion was on the couch, and I could hear the multi-audio from their OnBoard. When I was a kid and simmed too long that the day had passed I'd cry because I didn't have any more choices. It was still light, orange and purple against the walls, and I hoped they'd get up before it was dark.

Every time I felt myself rising to meet something we switched towns; an irony of my own making that socked me before any real revelation. Yes, there was something I was supposed to learn out there, but it stalled. Instead we moved on and I never saw anything again and was left with whatever I had taken in. I remembered less than I wanted — wanted to go back and map every stone so I could read the tea leaves, see where it was all going. Cleo set my eyes forward. Taught me that nothing mattered but that point between my eyes. And things became so sharp they lost sense. It was all window dressing to the Path. There was always something forward. I realized going back was pointless, gone, and all that mattered was the point just ahead on the road, where sky met land. Yes, that was life, that was push, and pull was anything that drew my gaze: divine and right, but evermore moving to the point. I realized I had been too caught up on the window dressing, that that was precisely what made it slip away. If I kept my gaze forward, always forward, the rest blurred, dragged, lingered. Could finally taste it. Yet every time I did this a bug flew in my eye; banged my hand against the armrest; Willie Nelson jumped me; a plate crashed.

I was physical, and always would be. Denying it would resign me to a disconnect worse than death. A constant reach.

159

~

Yellowstone sat simply in my head ever since the sim in the Ranch. I'd never been and the name had power I knew was drawing me to it — the next stop. It was overrun, and closed off to the public, which Craig and crew taught me meant it was more open than ever.

I imagined an eclectic bunch out there, waiting to take in a stray, and this felt more real than any town. A largely silent community, save for soft hiking songs for yourself. The world would forget about us, then the Earth. It seemed like the only option; Orion made a fine ghost, but it wasn't my fate. I wanted the real quiet. It would start up again anyways, so why shouldn't there be some period separate from the madness. That mad summer heat that blinds and suffocates. If I could control it things might be different, but if I could I wouldn't want to, so I could either be battered around by those hot winds or sink back.

I called Danny to tell him my plan. He grunted the way I knew his concern. Mom knew I was a goner long ago and only asked I be safe.


It started last Christmas, or maybe the one before, when the snow was worse. Grant was snowed in so the church couldn't get to him with a ham, but he didn't think that should've made a difference because he had gifted Joyce a snowmobile and it wasn't the worst storm that year and it was Christmas for God's sake, when no one should be alone. So he stopped volunteering and built a fence and trained brambles to climb it because the McLean's cats liked to wander into his yard and lounge in the willow. Joyce went over to reconcile, which he welcomed and demanded the snowmobile back or three hundred dollars because he could have made that selling it. She returned it but left him out of the potluck. He was still invited, just wasn't allowed to bring anything. So he stopped attending service entirely and when people saw him he said he was the happiest he had ever been, that he finally had some time for himself.

But no one had seen him for a few weeks and his car was still in the driveway, the brambles so unruly the gate stayed rigid. So Clearview figured it was mine or Orion's job to get through and check on him, which I told Orion, who was disgusted.

"Fucking Christ. I hate people."

"I know, I know."

The vines were thick around the three beams of the fence. Woven through the lock in a tumbleweed, squishy and tight. Beyond the fence weeds overtook the walkway, breaking through to the concrete porch where ivy hung from the gutter. We stood a moment as if expecting the house to move now that we were still.

Orion yelled Grant's name, louder, louder. Kicked the gate hard, harder. There must've been cement blocks keeping it up, or something had rooted in the dead wood and was growing around it — *nurse logs.*

"Check around back," said Orion.

It was hot, my feet heavy through the prairie grass stretching five miles every way. Looking at the willow cooled things a bit, languid brushes over the pale-yellow clouds. I missed Spencer's trees. There was a back gate, opened to the fields. This sense of dread ever since they told us about Grant: roots unhinging the jaw, tied to the ground in frozen decay, wildflowers pushing through old scars. My red wrist pulsed. I considered closing the gate and telling Orion I didn't find anything.

They led the way through to the cracked side door. Inside was clean and spacious, the blinds drawn tight so we navigated with the light from our OnBoards. Orion ripped down the curtains in the living room, revealing a pair of swords above the mantle. They poked them, picked one up then tossed me the second, heavier than it looked. We rattled them against one another's once, twice, a little duel, before I rested mine while Orion moved on to the kitchen with the curve of the saber fitted against their neck. Photos were everywhere and I wondered who Grant was. There was one with an older woman that could've been him and his mom, but he wasn't in the photo with three men and a fish. Sons? None of them looked alike.

"The gate," said Orion. "We should be checking the fields." I tried to fit the curtain rod back in its place before we

162

left, until Orion got frustrated and told me to leave it, but I told them I knew they wouldn't be back to weed it out, and they waited outside while I made it dark again. Orion waited halfway between the house and the gate, started to the field when I emerged.

They swiped at the grass, missing most except the top inch, drifting blades back at me. There was a path leading from the gate, back to a tree line. We passed clumps of grass that Orion wound up and stabbed into. One was a deer carcass, sending us faster to the trees, shirts held to our noses. The sun kept burning and would never set.

We reached the cool of the forest, waited on its border. There was no sign of Grant, and it would get dark fast among the trees. We had done all we could, made our way back to the house.

"You know most people turn *me* away," said Orion.

"What?"

"I go to a claim and start to explain I'm here to help, but they turn me away usually. The job's declined."

"Why do you think?"

Orion stood a few yards ahead and hacked the radius in front of them. "Don't think they want to waste either of our times. Pretending I can help isn't going to do them or me any good."

"Some people appreciate it."

"Sure. I help them. But even they seem to know, you know?"

"Sure."

"No, you know."

"Yeah."

"They know it can't go back to normal. They let it get like that — crazy to think I'll fix it."

What do you need? I wanted to ask. Instead we closed the back gate and went to Orion's SUV. The willow shivered.

Rain cut to the root of everything, infecting the air. Dirt, and mud, and phlegm. I wanted to vomit in solidarity. When I die, I hope it smells like that.

I pulled up on the day's last claim at 2:55pm. An oak fell through the roof, slanted to the left and back like a stick thrown in a bucket. The wind swayed its branches. A lapping against the shingles.

There was a car in the driveway, weeds circling the wheels — maybe two weeks since it was taken out.

I didn't grab any weedkiller or sheers. The door was cracked, grass growing in the light it let in. I poked it open further with my toe. The hole in the ceiling did nothing for the humidity. It was getting close. I circled the edge where light didn't touch, admiring the bulbous girth. The backrooms were well kept: a bedroom with the curtains drawn, a bathroom with plastic along the walls. It was getting close. I went back through the living room. Heard them before I saw them.

"The center of thingses what you're looking for," said Quinn Ruck. Their skull had a massive root popping through the top, the rest of them lost under the trunk. A hand reached to outside the circle of light, flowers cracking through the knuckles.

"Oh yeah?"

"Yeah. You have the right idea, most look out this way, but it's on the move — harder to kill that way." Damn. The rain had started.

"So how do you find it?"

Drops plinked through their hollow right cheek, a chuckle. "Never went looking. Ran into it on the Kansas border a while back. Always feel bad when I do because I know y'all are searching. Maybe that's why you don't though. Seems corny. Seems like I find it more than y'all though." A gust snapped through. They chuckled. "See? Might be some truth there." I sat on a root next to them and let my hair get wet. It felt good so slick.

Stepped out to the edge and touched my toes, left to right, right to left, stood and spun at the waist. Watched the drops slide down the bark. Left at 5:56pm.

I picked up linguine from Yates. Marijean seasoned her

chicken with paprika and parsley.

Her kitchen was soft in its lights and wood cutting boards and faded chestnut trims, and it reminded me winter came in more than snow. In there I felt the tide of the world roll over again and again like a note; enough that each meal was informed by its predecessor and the good ones were anticipated weeks ahead. Marijean worked with no OnBoard or music, that our conversation accented the noise rather than the reverse. I studied her slicing the chicken from the barstool.

"You cook growing up?" I asked.

"Me not so much. I'd help out my dad as a kid but didn't really start *cooking* until college. He made me miss something cooked yourself though. You?"

"A bit, the basics."

"Your mom cook much?"

"If she wanted to try something. But usually pasta."

Marijean's quiet was the best to sit in because it felt solid, holding you. It was in the air and went down in me until it was all the same frequency. Some were scared of this and needed to remind people they were people by making jokes or chattering. So when she motioned me over I delighted in not asking, simply sniffing what she held out. I rested my head in my arms and looked at the windowsill with its rag pile. These splotchy clouds walked from right to left, growing orange, purple, black. The world dropped off right then because there wasn't a single thing we had left to do but hadn't done a quarter of the things we wanted to; it was the end, and I wanted to rest for good, which might've happened if things were fair because why put someone through it all over again. People are people.

"You're sweet," said Marijean. I had felt her eyes on me just before.

"Thank you."

My favorite part was stepping out of the cave. I kept my head down on jobs, intent on tearing each weed. These walls of green I could go nuts on. Or I'd come in with weedkiller strapped to my back and coat the floor with that chemical stink, take a snow shovel and stroll along the floorboards, shaving off the lawn like dead skin. If anything really took root, maybe a shrub or sapling, I had a trowel in my back pocket I'd flip around and hammer into the dirt like an ice pick. Find the veins that always led to the heart: some gnarled bunch of roots supporting all the green. If it was too far down I might spend all day digging, seeing the clump but unable to get an angle on it. Those days I clocked out agitated. I'd walk home still turning the system over in my head, this puzzle box that always had the same answer. The next day I first had to clear out all the new growth. They had domain over the living room, considered me a minor setback. So I tore it all up again and reminded the homeowner how thorough they would have to be: pacing the room, making use of each sunlit crevice. *I can't keep the whole house moving.* But it was the only thing that stopped them. Then I got them out and was back for the real thing. The heartbeat of the room. More roots grew where I'd cut, and I was ready for them, had taken the night imagining an old shape. It was always easier the next day. I'd get under and around the thing and could lift it up like a fish on a hook, dripping dirt into the hole. Sweat on my forehead cool as I stepped out to the backyard and threw the thing as far as I could. I wondered if they had any sense of home, if they might try and make it back to the living room, but my job was done. And there was the exit. The sky opening on clean air; infinite to what I had known. Exhaled to hear it fade. I laughed because it was sunny and the clouds looked cliché. I sent over the report walking to the next job, remembering like a dream the boiler room and its millions of pressure valves to poke and prod, shook my head at how silly it was that I took it so seriously when there was so much *more*.

Montana slept in the memory of summer nights. The wind whipped all the green around until it screamed. Cars moved slow lest they get grabbed by a ditch, buried.

I had worked a path from the back of the house through some fields to a roadside spot that served doubles right; the brush became forgiving after the first clearing, opening to pewter grass fields. My ears rang in the brief respites — the quiet every

168

living thing left behind. It felt close; it might've been, out on the curling sea. I sat in the grey, feeling the wind might spin me up.

I had never expected the world to retreat. I told Mom we knew, we knew it all, and we would learn every atom. But we were smarter and left it. We figured it was too much, knew when we were beat. We knew our world; the complexity of which was miniscule in comparison. The breeze paused. Nothing stirred for fear of mistake. Dew perspired in the valleys of grass. I imagined my head slammed into the dirt, down, down, cracking my spine, legs in a bent Y. I knew I didn't need to drink but still wanted to, so when the bar was closed, I laughed.

I took the same way back. They were onyx fields then, sinking to caverns left long ago, and I knew no one was coming, finally.

I messaged Sci. They got to know Nebraska and its sandhills, the endless ones that ate people even before Overgrowth. Nomads shambled from one castaway to the next, insatiable over a find like Sci, so when they had to leave there were proposals abound, of lives simple and grand, in exchange for a company Sci had never known the absence of.

It was more disco than they expected. Thedford, where they'd been the longest, communicated with their neighbors through fireworks. It was like being out at sea. Winds shifted grasses, shifted the town, so they stayed in on bad days and watched kids kitesurf from the windows. It was a group of five with sleds on their feet that floated over the sea, skidding across shingles, bouncing back up as cartoons against the sky, touching down, parting the prairie grass like a comb. They were hometown kids back from California for the summer. Sci tried a couple times and almost broke their neck. What they didn't tell you until you were strapped in was you kept going until the wind gave out — that they'd use a tracker to pick you up, even if it was only the corpse.

"You're just ragdolling through the fields," I laughed.

"I know right! Morbid."

Science hadn't changed so neither had they, making my dissection all the more intriguing. This uprooting of theirs: questions, innocuous, cutting to the root of my being, so they felt the Ranch and Blaze Team and the rain and oak house, and the weight that might've crushed us at the fairground.

I told them about getting to drive the peanut truck. They laughed. "I missed you."

"Missed you too."


The rain always cleared to an ember of sky: sometimes a single blazing dot on a map of baby blue, then a cauldron of supernova braided through the clouds. Faded to night, where things were quiet and simmering in the wet. Balmy balmy, windows open for some puff to roll through the house. I laid naked on top of my bed — sheets, pillows, and blankets long gone. The fan only pushed hot air around. And it made me chuckle. I kissed the air, blew it out the window.

I traced my finger along the curve of the mattress; mirrored the one in my elbow. The red looked like a scar in the grey light. Felt its raised edges. My left hand raised it to me; kissed. Too early to sleep. A string of light was under my door, and I could hear chatter.

All the overhead lights were on as they never had been, and for a moment it looked like a normal home with its golden wood blanks and granular walls. The shrubs mistaken for houseplants if I softened my gaze. Orion was on the couch, projecting something. It took a second to recognize them both. They were in separate parts of my mind, but I suppose they always knew each other. Rachel dove in the opposite direction of the soccer ball; Grayson yelled at her for going easy, that they actually wanted to get better, and Rachel laughed like I'd never seen her.

Orion smiled softly behind the OnBoard. They texted Rachel back in Spencer and had forgotten to tell me.

I crossed my legs on the other side of the couch. Orion teased their hands around Willie Nelson's head and snapped them back as she reached. I watched a bit of that and the kids playing, stretched my back around the arm of the couch, listened to the jowls flap and *Oh yeah? C'mon. Almost, almost!* She barked

171

but Orion was louder and she calmed. I sighed, sprung up. Orion was wide eyed at me and I chuckled.

"What?" They laughed.

"I don't know," I said.

A phantom closed the space. Another life, perhaps. Decided to ride it. Stepped up.

"Goodnight." I walked off.

"Night." Slightest hitch. I felt like Orion.


Most people left us alone once they saw our duo. There weren't many claims left so I took time on what I had. Sci reviewed notes. We talked less because we knew more.

One little blur was the Milky Way, a dot near the couch. The center, above the coffee table, was a blinding orb. Back by the wall, pinpricks floated around like fireflies, teasing some existence beyond myself. Then everything flew by, zooming into the Milky Way, then the Sun, so Neptune grew from my chest. Sci zoomed back out, to a nearby Goldilocks planet, described the distance in hundreds of years at our top speed, getting from the foyer to the couch, that cryogenics were ridiculous but the simplest answer so far. Then back out to the Milky Way, its blinding black hole of a center thousands, millions of years away, foyer to the coffee table. Then back to the universe, unfathomable time, intelligent life evolving and destroying itself, from the couch to the coffee table.

"What're these?" I asked. A cluster of stars webbing together.

"The plant's making it look more significant than it is," said Sci. The fern gave shape to the light folds. "It's a superheated cluster that formed just after the Big Bang. See that deadzone over there?" On the other side of the room where the wall met the ceiling, dark. "That's its counterpart."

"How do we know it's there?"

"Well 'cause we know the cluster's over there, and we don't see much the other way."

"Science is all one-to-one, huh?"

They shrugged. "Makes sense. There's fire, there's water. Extremes can't exist without an opposite."

"Is that a scientific fact?"

"Alright, alright. I'm just saying we haven't seen an instance without it. From biology to quantum mechanics. And if there isn't, it's usually because a body exists in both spaces simultaneously."

"Quantum." I thought about us in Spencer. I asked, "Do you like having a body?"

"What?"

"Like if you could not have one, would you?"

"Never known a life without one."

"Sure you do. You're in a sim and going, you forget you're in a room. My mom used to say that about books."

173

"Oh, so like living in a sim?"

"I guess. Or like what you do now, but without the sleeping, eating, injuries, you know."

"I don't think it works like that."

"I know, it's a hypothetical."

"No, like, none of it would mean anything. My whole thing is that I do have to piss and shit and sleep. It's annoying, but if I didn't, I wouldn't be me, so I can't answer your question."

Cleo told me about their name on one of those long drives for sun. He had the wheel because part of the drive was driving and I even found myself missing it, the dull focus. "Cleo" wasn't "Cleopatra," nor a mermaid, nor a new name, but a distillation of gibberish; kaleidoscope, kaleidoscope, kaleedoscoop kaleedo kaleeo kleeo one trivia night back east. Their ex convinced them to go with the "C" for ease, and he since regretted that but didn't want to go through the whole process again for a couple letters.

At the edge of the night Clearview's old world crept in and beat me over the head with death, and bubbled back to the beginning to go through it all again, and die and bubble. It sounded like a baritone, with the only beat from my blood. Things rustled and howled or snorted nearby, but they could smell some fragility and stayed to themselves. Nowhere I went was quiet until I made it so, and then I could be anywhere. I tried new trails or walked off them. But finding a way back was simple.

Once in Wynne, I got excited being miles from downtown, in the thickets off a field off a dirt road that led nowhere. Dotted leaves dripped around, letting in the crescent of moonlight. Grass grabbed and begged me to lie down. I broke into a grove with a roof poking out the other side, and I knew there would be a road and I'd never be lost.

There was a rustling to the left. I saw ears first, then focused on its pyramid face, the wide, set eyes staring at me. I thought of Orion's description — *potatoes with legs.* Yates charged them on the road because they were everywhere without wolves, which Sci said we were trying to bring back because deer were spreading a nasty tick, but ticks seemed better than wolves. Sci considered the whole thing though; I just liked to walk.

A baby edged away, closer to its mom. There were a couple. I took a breath and waved, pointed the way I was moving. They watched me until I reached the outside of the grove. A clean breeze blew at my back, and I pressed my fingers to my lips, held them up in farewell.

Someone showed up at the house, which scared me because I hadn't thought that they all knew where we lived on the job, but then again there were only so many people in town and when a new car kept rolling around they must have noticed.

Miranda Pulok had an urgent request to deal with a property just outside of town. The doorbell had rung for a while and I was determined not to answer it because I had taken the day off and I knew Orion was in the living room, but they let it keep ringing and ringing and ringing, maybe because they knew I'd answer it, and of course I did, so I was on the hook to drive with Miranda to some barn ten miles away.

She told me about her family and how the rest of them had moved out after Overgrowth. Which was typical of them, because that's always how they handled things, leaving her in the lurch, to deal with things like the family barn. Not like anyone had asked her to deal with it, but if she didn't no one would and her great-grandpa had built the thing by hand so how could she let it devolve into a giant greenhouse. Oh well, she liked it out there anyways. The nights were cool and she could go out onto her patio with her husband and smoke a cigarette late with all the lights off and they couldn't see a thing for miles except the stars above, so the patio table and their faces were this deep blue fading to black, until they puffed and you could see a little orange on their noses, a light in the eyes.

The barn was at the other end of Clearview from her place, so she couldn't keep up with the maintenance as much as she wanted to, and when she went back that weekend she noticed the creep along the west wall and how they eroded the support beams. There was nothing in there of value, but her great-grandpa had built the thing by hand and she couldn't let it fall apart because of our negligence. Miranda pulled up to the white barn and moaned. It was already tilting. I couldn't tell, but she had seen it since she was a little girl. They had barbeques out there — the whole family when they were still around. So I went in and gazed up like I was in church because trees inside had made their own buttresses, spanning the distance from eave to eave to hold the rotted white wood with a green skeleton. *Nurse log.* I approached a beam, poked through to the wood which felt squishy compared to the bone of vines that surrounded it.

"I think it's gone," I said.

"What?"

"Like, the barn is more these plants than anything. If you cut them all out the planks would fall and it'd be over."

Miranda tilted back, looked around. "I don't think so."

I wanted to burn the thing down, just to show her. Take out the support trunks first so the white roof would fall into the pyre.

"Listen," she said. "My husband knows construction. I'm going to bring him around and you two can figure something out."

"I don—"

"He built our home. No offense, but he definitely knows more about this than you." And she got in her car and left me there.

177

I waited just inside the door until the sun tilted, when my shadow was longer than me, then I stepped out. On all sides were neglected fields. The gravel at the mouth of the barn reminded me of the beach, how it softened. The cicadas sang. A peace felt for generations. Two, three hours by then? I started toward the cracked asphalt. Salt in my mouth as the sweat dripped. Raised my hand through my hair, flicked it down to the ditch. In it there was an echo. Yes, it had happened before, somewhere else, would happen again. And I was grateful for it. Singular.

But it stretched, and I knew it would never end. The sun fell, the sweat froze on my skin. Miles to go. I almost hailed the first car I saw, but remembered I'd left my OnBoard at the house, that no one knew where I was, and jumped into the brush instead. Maybe one of them was Miranda, coming back. That hope passed.

I hadn't walked out that far, was frustrated I hadn't, like I was supposed to have an internal map of every town. A sign reflected off the moonlight — barely a crescent — "Clearview 2 miles."

And I remembered having a partner. Banished the thought. But it crept along the edges until I was enveloped in grace. Leaving half the world to mystery. To lean. Push and pull.

Blowing through town after town was why I was here. To see and move. But I was caught. Made docile. Aware it was a trick. Again and again it would come, to tease, then enrage, then despair. Powerless to script. Because nothing changed. Miranda was Yates of a different ilk, mixed and matched. And the moment I thought I could pin it, it slipped. If I could feel them on the beach, space between, warmed by sun, I would know the chasm. I had never felt nor would ever feel anything new, only forget. But so I would forget this. And I focused my eyes on the road ahead, the sway of branches, felt certain the noise behind me was not natural. Then what is natural? The humidity maybe. Walking through soup. Sweat had thawed.

Orion. Three points for a belt. Where did they sit in the constellation? It was all the same. And when the last of the stars flew out to the edge of the universe all would be still. That was death: top of breath. Little death, the eternal, the recurring. All leading to one. A car blared behind me and I jumped to the ditch. I had been walking right down the center.

There were these generator lights the town kept going near the entrance to main street. The only lights for miles. And it was like that I found my way home. I couldn't remember any streetlights in Wynne or Spencer. I remembered the paths though. Remembered my favorite parts; like in Wynne when I was getting close to the creek but couldn't see it yet, only smell the mud. The trail then wound into the creek so I was walking the slope. I didn't know how old a runoff so small could be, but I liked to imagine generations seeing the same things I saw. So there must be someone else that walked to the lights like that, moving out of the black.

I looked down at my wrist one day and it was gone. When did I stop checking? Why did I ever? The groove had felt comfortable, an impression I could trace wherever my fingers rested. Not even a scar left. There had been pride in exposing it to the world, making everyone see the ugly red thing, but then again, no one had ever said anything. I wished someone else had felt the heat.

I dreamt those days. Kris hung on the outside of things. Maybe she knew the power she had over the house. I slid against the wall next to her and she smiled. I wanted nothing more than to keep her eyes on me. And she asked me questions. Genuinely wanted to know, and there I was laughing too much. So I focused on the scene around us and remembered my place. I wanted to ask her something serious, and she knew and didn't mind.

"How long have you and Wells been together?"

"There was some on and off in the beginning. We've known each other for twenty-four years this October."

I told her what Cleo had said.

"Hahaha, yes, I suppose it is a show sometimes. For ourselves more than anyone though. It's good to know someone's willing to put on an act for the sake of it, you know."

"What about Simon?"

"What about him?"

"You could drift apart. Divide over him." Kris shrugged.

"Maybe. I don't think so though."

"Why?"

Her laugh was always for herself. "We're not the same people as when we met. I've gotten used to waking up to someone new. There's a core I suppose that brought us together, and that helps, but if I cling to that then I'll lose him and everyone else for sure."

Kris didn't think Simon and Orion should be together. *Separate, outlying wavelengths.*

Wells thought they shared something.

She preferred Simon with Germaine, whose room he'd been lingering in, when everyone else retired and they remained. Chatting away until one nodded, then the other.

"Hey, we should grab a drink," said Sci.

"Yes!" It was my last weekend.

On my way to the bar, the peanut sailed past, pulled off in front of me. They were blowing by for the night, wanted to see the town, had stories to tell. I pinged Sci an apology and said we should try tomorrow.

Kari was playing music while Jake drove. She switched to something up-tempo, syncopated, room to move in between the beat.

"Oh stop!" Jake shook his head, then flicked a hand out, down, sung over his shoulder. Kari howled and picked it up. I could feel Dale dancing behind me in how the peanut shivered. I'd never heard the song but recognized everything else, how the heart swelled; it was the first thing I'd ever heard.

"'Small Joys' is the theme," said Kari. She was behind the wheel. "Usually we contact a mayor or sheriff, and if they're into it they get a bunch of folks ready. Dale sends the drone out ahead of time so you can see them see it, which is a lot of fun. Some people cry! Kids love it most. They just want to get in here and sit behind the wheel. We get some testimonials: how hard it's been, having us as a constant."

"Kinda bullshit," said Jake.

"Oh my god, yes, we get it," said Kari.

"Ok, but it's true. Planters helped fund the experiments that fucked this up."

"Ok. So?"

"So, they're literally giving *peanuts*— and yes! I know, I know about the Little Seed Fund. Still pennies compared to how much they fucked it up."

"So they give everything away and we don't have jobs?"

"I'd have a different job!"

"Sure, so would everyone. We don't *need* peanuts. Play the 'if' and 'should' card all you like."

"Ugh, I know, I know, ok?" He sulked in the back for a while. This rift that sat between them, that Dale stepped around. If he didn't do that dance, could they still get along? Would they grind against each other, with no distraction, no other energy to bring them out of it? An ache in my chest. The thought that they were dependent on one another, that it was actually just a house of cards they didn't know they were maintaining. Did I think it into existence? I ran my hand along the ridges of the shell. Let it go, let it go.

"Are there any other Nuts on the road?" I asked. There used to be three: East, Mid, and West. But the other two weren't as popular anymore, so it was just them. I took the four of us to the spot where the bowling league drank because it was the cheapest. It was still light when we got in so I didn't have to see the spot with no stars where I drowned.

Dale went to New Orleans for Mardi Gras two years ago and swears he saw the origin of the atom. From Canal Street there was a curtain of vines hiding Billows that once he stepped through cut him off from all sounds in this world. Swathes of trees condensed the road to a tunnel, wrapping ruddy trunks leading him through. His friends hadn't seen him turn off, so he pressed on, pulled by the symmetry of the way. A salon blown out with bushes was halfway between where he had entered and the walled green at the end; these turned-over pink upholstered chairs rocked as if to comfort themselves, but the bark around

183

promised a calmer end. The cash in the register was out of date. There was a mattress in the back, still white. Now maybe it was the seclusion of this street or the melancholy of the salon but Dale took a nap there.

Kari beat him on the shoulder at this.

"Oh just wait," said Dale.

"Fucking men."

When he awoke a grey-bearded man blocked the door to the exit, leaning on his left hip, right hand in his pocket. Dale could tell he was off balance. Dale apologized, for sleeping in what he assumed was this guy's bed. But the guy laughed and slid down against the wall. He owned the place, had left the mattress there for his sister, whenever she came around. Dale had tripped the sensor and he hoped it was her.

"I can't keep anything good here." The man said. "Wanna get somewhere we can get a drink?"

"No, I like it here," said Dale.

New Orleans was busier than ever those days, busier than Gabriel had seen it anyways, pervaded though by insects who flew in, fed, flew on. And it had always been like that, but when he walked around back in the day there was a knowing look between natives — they knew the real secrets. Now there were hidden places closed off to them, yet yielded to drunkards in masks. Dale knew he was one of them. So the city became smaller for its inhabitants and an artifice for tourists. It was sifting them out, punishing complacency.

Gabriel's sister, Adeline went up to Baton Rouge to hold the line. He thought it was a fresh start for her, some discipline. See, she had been in and out of clinics — opioids — but nothing really lasts and he caught wind she'd come back down to the city, told her a dozen times about this spot where he wouldn't bug her. She must've figured that was a crock of shit because there he was. See, every time he tried to do something it made things worse. Like reminding Adeline she had a place kept her from using it. And the more he wanted to learn the new city the more it shut itself up.

"I told Gabriel, 'I think you're overthinking it,'" said Dale. "And he said, 'Well what else am I supposed to think about?' and I couldn't tell him, but didn't seem like he needed to think of anything you know? So we did get a drink and by the end I could see what he was actually like, but I could tell having such a good time only reminded him of everything else getting at him, so what can you do?"

"What did you do?" I asked.

He shrugged. "We ended the night. Got his number, reached out a few months ago, but he never responded."

The next day Sci was busy with a remote conference, and I had to pack, so Sunday we met up for breakfast where they told me about a lizard that cleans its asshole with its tongue and I wouldn't believe them until we were pressed together in the booth watching the video. When it finished, they looked down at my wrist.

"So, what's next?" said Sci.

"Orion's trying to be out by noon."

"Ah damn. I wanted to show you something."

"Oh I'm sure you'll send me plenty."

"Yeah, you're pretty dumb," they said. "But no, it's this spot to wait out the rain. I got caught there last week and thought you'd like it."

"Where at?"

"Nah, you've got to get going."

"Yeah yeah." They smelled like cedarwood.


Orion wasn't in at noon, and none of their luggage was ready. I wanted to message Sci about the spot. That pull again, the one I'd learned to ignore. I leashed Willie Nelson for a walk. We went along the main road with its pools, which she had to inspect for tadpoles, straining the leash so that her front paws floated over the murk. Rain clouds marched on a worn afternoon — typical of departures. Typical of October. Nelson chased Orion's car as much as she could while they waved.

"Thanks for taking her out."

"No problem."

We were on the road to D.C. as the first drops fell. A

186

path cleaved through the dead brush out of town, out of the rain. We hardly noticed the roll of North Dakota in our familiar silence. Finally the heat had ended and all the green withered to orange then brown as we had made it another year and could sleep.

We started looking for a motel when the sun was in the rearview. The change in west to east hadn't hit until then. Foliage looked frail in the fading light. I grabbed Gary Jr. to see whether any leaves had changed, but they looked the same.

I dreamt. A mass of dirt chased me across the plain while Orion watched. The ground slid out from underneath so I angled up and I wanted to sit back like I was in the Mustang and blast out of there but it flipped me over and I was falling through the bottom of the earth into space. Yates, from the ether, kept repeating I should have watched it. I got upset thinking about floating out there forever and ever and wished I'd died.

Willie wasn't in the car the next morning. Orion had given her to the motel owner after he took a liking to her. It was as good a place as any, and she was happy anywhere.

"What happened the other week anyways?" asked Orion.

"What do you mean?"

"When you came in looking like shit."

"Oh."

"Yeah, 'oh.'"

"This idiot I met was in town. Got us beat in some bar."

They chuckled. "You'll throw in with anyone, huh?"

"I wouldn't say that." I didn't like what they saw in it.

"Sure, sure." They were driving us until Minneapolis. "Alright, I should mention: I slept with Sci the other night."

I lurched forward and laughed. "You fucker."

"I know." They laughed. "They told me not to tell you at least."

"Oh my god, you're the worst."

"Hahaha. They were shitfaced, going on and on about particle matter."

"Particulate." I shook my head, smiling wide at the narrow clouds.

I went over to Yates' place one time. It was after work, after he'd closed the store, and I'd stopped by because it was mid-April and getting nice enough that I just wanted to be around people. He had a couple of js he'd been meaning to get rid of, so why not. It was a ranch just outside of Wynne proper with lawn gnomes and imported flamingos, *the Florida ones are cheaper and a brighter pink than anywhere!* It smelled like cat and I worried for a moment that Orion would pick up on it. But why did I care? So I sat back in the recliner and let Bubba climb on top of me while Yates sparked up. He hadn't smoked in a while so he was all giggly. I sat back and stroked Bubba. The place reminded me of my grandma's — all wood and paper. I reached down to feel the carpet and found it was exactly how it looked. That white curly stuff. The cats got a kick out of scratching it. Tufts pulled up everywhere.

Yates held his head while he stood up. *Steaks.* He had steaks in the freezer. I moved to get up with him but he pressed his hand to the air between us — I was a guest. Bubba was purring anyways, so I let myself be served. There wasn't anything about his living room I didn't already know. Why had I expected more than the man he presented?

We got to the wastelands of Wisconsin, past the Twin City burn teams. The black of night foreboding with its distant forests that threatened to take up Overgrowth and march across the plain to smother you in your sleep. The day streaked as if begging for this time to be different, for the leaves to stay burnt, above ash. Our rooms were next to each other for the first time since March. Orion invited me for a movie just as I was getting ready for bed.

They wore only loose shorts as they died their hair in the tub — mahogany. I was on the luggage holder browsing through my OnBoard for something to screen.

"I got your favorite," they said. The bottle was the same color as their new hair.

"I'm trying to be clear for the way back."

They chuckled. "Oh right." And poured two tall glasses.

It was after our fourth drink that we thought it better to skip the movie. I reached for the bottle, and they seized my forearm, saying how big it was. A hard summer, I said. *Yeah yeah.* They kneaded the veins, and I wanted to rip it away but felt my fingers flex, activated.

They told me about their favorite job this season: a farmer who insisted on helping to the point he was the one doing all the work.

"He couldn't stand me hacking the way I was," said Orion. Holding my arm. "Like he *knew* I was doing it wrong, but was too polite to tell me so, and too helpful to let it keep going like that."

"Wow, wow."

"Good guy. Swear you only find them out there."

"You going straight from D.C. to Florida?"

Orion looked at the ground and giggled and shrugged. Let go. "Not winter yet."

The room got cold and I wondered if that made any difference; if Florida's heat wrapped around and around, crashing them into it. They kicked me a couple times while I laid on the carpet, their chest rippling.

"If you're sleeping here, it's in the bed. No point in the rug."

"Right, right." And I sloshed over to the covers where

190

they crawled in and we slept.

I got up in the fading warmth of September. It was Sunday, and Sci had an excursion planned for us. There was some propulsive quality to them that made my days lounging in the grass or wandering the roads seem ridiculous. So I felt us spinning faster and the old impulse to slip away rose from gut to chest. When it reached my head I remembered pewter caverns and instead moved to dress.

Sci waited in the driveway for me, glasses shaded under the light. I tapped the window to invite them in for breakfast: four eggs, turkey bacon, and mango.

"Really living it up these days."

"Oh you know me."

I pinged Orion but they stayed in their room.

On the way out they told me more about Nebraska and its dust. It reminded me of this carpenter's place I cleared, which reminded them of a cool chair they'd had in their room, and so on until we were in Wyoming. Warped to a world of ochre slopes mossed with pines.

"So what's Oklahoma?" I asked

"South, obviously."

"What?! Are you out of your mind?"

"Yes! But that doesn't have to do with this."

"It's prairies, and beige, and a musical."

"Cowboys! Oil. Texas. Grits." We talked over each other.

"Obviously categories are useless," said Sci.

"No, we need to nail it down."

"Naturally."

The road up was beaten brush that *fwupped* under the sedan, bouncing us until it wasn't funny. We pulled off and got out where it turned to grassy slopes. A shelf across the valley reflected the sun on our hill in the middle of nowhere. I fit my hand to theirs.

We made D.C. the day after next. Howard thanked us for a job well done and informed us that the program was done as there was no point in paying reps to go out to abandoned areas, and Orion grew tight. There was a bonus I hadn't known about, paid in one bump to my last paycheck that might buy me a new OnBoard.

My friend had reinvested each of my paychecks and made a good deal. I chatted with them on the train to Overbrook and learned I could take the year off if I wanted. Guess that's what a season of free housing got. An image of a ghost floating over the plains came to mind.

The ride back was surprising in how weeded it felt. After eight months in the jungle, I'd expected to see nothing but concrete and waste. Instead, my eyes slipped to the edges and spaces between leaves, the ribbing of trunks, shrub formations. Even litter felt purposeful in how the wind had settled it, millions of nodes stretched impossibly thin, and moving through it all was like pushing water. Suddenly I was giddy. I laughed and shook my head. A lilt I'd never heard.

The train drifted past lakes framed in orange, the water silver against the sky. No more bob and weave, just a straight line. There was a stink about me I liked. I smelled every piece, taking in the smoke and pollen and air, oh the air.


Danny picked me up from the station and we hugged. His silence felt like Marijean's and I realized I missed him. *Mom wants you to come by.* We passed a cedar tree on the way to his place that we always passed on the way to swim lessons when we were kids and it was still the most solid thing I had ever known. It annoyed me no one had tried making a treehouse out there, but I supposed I had only seen a fraction of a fraction, and I was sad the program ended despite having no desire to go back, with still no desire to stay. Danny described a few weeks in South Carolina and their new islands with lapping waves and I wanted to cry because it was exactly what he should have done.

"Souvenir?" asked Danny.

"A gift." I put Gary Jr. on the windowsill. He let me crash on his couch while I searched for something else. We put on cartoons and smoked the first night. I got up off the couch with the slanting grey light, contemplating a month. But I was still hungry, so I walked a few miles for supplies and came back with pasta. Danny laughed when he saw me chopping tomatoes, and I laughed with him. We ate while the kitchen stunk of roasted garlic early, early that noon. It was Saturday, which had meaning for me again. He said I looked quiet, and I chuckled because I never felt louder. He left for a buddy's birthday that afternoon while I searched for a job, then when he came back we cooked and got ready for another day.

# Acknowledgements

Thank you Andre Zielinski for being the first person to ever pay me for my writing. You are a gifted educator and inspiration for the arts.

Mom, Dad, Maggie, Hannah, Sarah, JP, Mary — in my prayers every night. Thank you especially Mom and Sarah for being the first to read, and Dad for being a paid subscriber of my Substack. This wouldn't have been a production without Lily Schneiderman kicking my ass. Thank you.

Thank you Clay Wilson, Karrah Goldberg & Lily for the love. Greenpoint is nothing without you.

Elena Koufis, the first copy I got I signed for you, as promised.

Adam, Javen, Tyler, Octo, Natalie, Shelby, Izzy, Emily, Alec & Mike, I'd give you one big collective kiss if I could.

No Name Writing Group — who's next?

Thank you Bushwick Writers Group for helping me finish.

Thank you Red Shed Community Garden for green.

Finally, thank you Charlotte Grimm for making *Overgrown* beautiful.

## Luke Madden

A Midwest kid living in Brooklyn —
pro-magic, pro-cook, and pro-walk.
lukelore.substack.com
written1999.com